CYNTHIA MELTON

Deema

The Fate of the Faes, book 2

By Cynthia Melton

Copyright © 2018 by Cynthia Hickey/Cynthia Melton

Published by Take Me Away Books, an imprint of Winged Publications

All rights reserved. No part of this publication may be resold, reproduced, stored in a retrieval system, or transmitted in any form or by any means, electronic, mechanical, recording, or otherwise, without the prior written permission of the author. Piracy is illegal. Thank you for respecting the hard work of this author.

This is a work of fiction. All characters, names, dialogue, incidents, and places either are the product of the author's imagination or are used fictitiously. Any resemblance to actual events, locales, or people, living or dead, is entirely coincidental.

All rights reserved.

ISBN-13: 978-1-0881-3911-0

DEDICATION

To all those who tirelessly fight the battle between
Good and Evil

Character List:

Faeries

Shayna
Deema
Queen Linette
Earin
Alvar
Queen Brigette

Humans

Pierce Cochran
Clark Payson
Luke Marshal
Hanna
Logan

Other races

Kasdeya – demon
Abaddon – Leader of the dark
Radella – vampire
Seamus – Leprechaun
Paddy – Leprechaun
Gorna – dragon
Dragona - dragon
Agatha – witch
Linc – Shifter – panther

1
Deema

The most recent battle dispelled some of the darkness encroaching on the human world, but not enough to restore the day to its full brightness. Scientists couldn't explain the phenomena, quieting people's questions with vague answers of climate change as dusk fell earlier each day. But Deema could explain it all.

She took one last glance at the sky and stepped through the portal and home. It filled her with joy to be allowed back after her past bad decisions.

The faeries had done well in the battle against Kasdeya's minions, but not a day went by that the air in The Glen didn't ring with the clash of swords in preparation for the next battle. With Abaddon freed from his chains, another battle was imminent, and the side for the Light needed more warriors.

Deema headed straight for the infirmary where

Queen Linette struggled to bounce back after suffering a slice to her shoulder from a poisoned blade. Shayna fought her own uphill battle to recover from her injuries. After suffering a vampire bite, she'd been drained of her blood. The only remedy—the blood was thoroughly cleansed, then added back into her body—not an easy or unpainful task. In the meantime, guarding New York City had fallen on Deema's shoulders, and she wanted to give the task back to Shayna immediately.

She paused in the doorway of the infirmary and held her breath as Queen Linette handed her staff to Shayna. "I place The Glen and those of the fae world into your hands, Shayna. I may not regain my full strength and must use what little I have to oversee the production of new chains to bind Abaddon."

"No, my queen." Shayna stepped back, letting the staff fall to the marble floor with a clatter. "I cannot."

"You must." The queen fell onto a mound of pillows. "I leave our people in good hands. Use—" She caught sight of Deema. "Ah, there she is. Come, my dear." She held out a trembling hand. "You must work by Shayna's side as she once did mine. Keep her safe."

Deema grasped the queen's hand and bowed. "I will do all in my power not to disappoint." She choked back a sob. They wouldn't survive without their queen. All because of Radella, the vampire bound in the dungeon. The undead woman could stay there for eternity as far as Deema was concerned.

"Good." The queen closed her eyes. "I leave in two days' time whether I am well or not. Evil waits for no one. Go, I must rest."

Deema picked up the staff and handed it to Shayna. "You can do this."

She shook her head, her eyes swimming with tears. "It isn't my place. I wasn't born to rule."

"It is your place. For a time, at least." She closed Shayna's fingers around the staff. "I will help you." She bowed. "My queen."

A sob escaped Shayna. "Do get up. We will reign together."

Deema glanced up. "Already the light around you glows brighter." She smiled. "Just don't let it go to your head."

Shayna gave a shuddery laugh. "I'm sure you will keep me in my place. Shall we let our friends know?" Her eyes widened. "Am I allowed to leave this place?"

Queen Linette chuckled. "You are queen. You may do as you please as long as matters are cared for here first. The Glen is your top priority." She waved a weak hand. "I know I handed over my staff, but I did ask you to leave so I may rest."

"We'll go." Deema gave Shayna a nudge toward the door, eager to see Clark Payson, her favorite of the three human detectives who help the fae.

Faerie after faerie bowed as the two walked by. The staff Shayna clutched in her hand was all they needed to know the reign of power rested with another.

At the entrance to the portal, Shayna stopped and glanced at the staff. "I cannot take this with me, can I?"

Deema shrugged. "Maybe it turns into something else in the human world. Let's see."

With a nod, Shayna stepped into the portal and came out in Central Park in New York City. She now clutched a blue umbrella and laughed. "Not a cloud in the sky, and I'll have to carry this. Doesn't go with the whole Special Agent façade, does it?"

"Humans are strange creatures. You'll get a look or two and nothing more." Deema grabbed her hand and teleported them to Shayna's hotel room where the witch, Agatha, engaged in her favorite pastime. Watching talk shows on television.

Agatha glanced up. "You're back. It's good to see you." She flashed a snaggle-toothed grin. "What's on the agenda for today?" Her gaze fell on the umbrella in Shayna's hand and widened. She flicked off the television and bowed her head. "Queen."

"Please don't put on any pretenses for me. I'm not your queen."

"But you are a queen. Did Linette die?"

"No, she's occupied with other things. Let's visit the precinct, shall we? I need to let Pierce know of this change."

"Most definitely." Agatha changed into a large rottweiler and stood still while Shayna clipped a leash around her neck. Purely pretense, as it usually trailed on the ground behind them, but humans jumped back in fear when they caught sight of the large, unleashed dog.

Deema's best friend might now rule the fae world, and she would be stretched between ridding the human world of darkness and ruling the world of the fae, but she was still Shayna, warrior of the Light. For this, Deema was grateful. There was no other warrior as powerful except for Alvar, the traitor.

Rather than teleport to the precinct and shock those who didn't know who they really were, Deema hailed a cab. The driver cast a wary glance at Agatha, but allowed them inside the vehicle. Agatha bared her teeth and leaped into the front passenger seat.

Deema laughed. She loved the feisty, ancient witch who enjoyed terrifying others but had a warrior's heart.

Shayna

Reigning queen. Shayna's insides quivered. She'd thought being the queen's top warrior was a challenge.

While Deema went to find Payson, and Agatha plopped down in the staff lounge to intimidate the uniformed officers, Shayna stopped in Pierce's doorway and watched him. He sat with his back to the door, phone to his ear. She loved this man with every fiber of her being. Just when she'd made the choice to bind herself to him after the final battle was fought, she became queen. Now was not the time for further entanglements, nor was it allowed.

"I told you to take care of the dispute earlier this morning! If a woman is hurt because of your incompetence, I'll feed your head to Agent Sky's dog." He slammed the receiver down and turned, his face breaking into a grin. Without hesitation he got to his feet, pulled her further into the room, and closed the door. "You're here."

"I am." She leaned into him as his arms folded around her. "I've missed you."

"I've been busy." He tilted her face to his. "Are you all right? I've stopped in The Glen every day at the infirmary, but most times you were sleeping."

"I'm fine, but you may want to sit down." She gave a trembling smile.

"Okay." He resumed his seat, folding his hands on his desktop while Shayna sat across from him.

She took a deep breath. "Queen Linette handed over her staff."

He sat back. "To whom?"

"Me."

He paled. "You're the fae queen?"

She nodded.

"How do I act? Do I bow?"

"If you do I'll strike you with my staff." She held up the umbrella. "Don't treat me any different. Just think of it as an added responsibility loaded onto my already-heavy shoulders."

"A rather large responsibility." He laughed, his eyes twinkling. "I'm now the chief of police, and you're the queen. Watch out, worlds." His smile faded. "I can't help but think this doesn't bode well for our relationship."

"It—"

"Chief." The receptionist, another new one—this time a woman around the age of fifty and very competent instead of the empty-headed Barbie doll the chief had had in the past—interrupted via the phone intercom. "We've a riot outside. Shows promise of being nasty."

"And not human," Shayna said. She didn't need to look outside to know the trouble had started fresh upon her arrival.

"Thank you, Mary Ann." Pierce grabbed his jacket from the back of his chair.

He and Shayna joined the others in a rush toward the front doors. "They can't come in," Shayna said. "The holy water Pierce doused the place with before the battle will keep them away, but there are plenty of people in danger outside." Pedestrians were drawn to anything out of the ordinary and sometimes got in the way of their own protection. She glanced at Mary Ann. "Bolt these doors. Do not open them for any reason. If we need medical attention, we have phones."

"Officer Charges, keep the uniforms inside to protect the civilians. Let no one other than us five in until I flash my badge," Pierce said. "Understood?"

"But, sir, we can help."

"Not this time."

The click of the door signaled it locking behind them. She'd have to do some damage control with those in and out of the building after they cleared the sidewalk, but it wasn't the first time. Things would be much simpler if she could show her true race. "The rest of you stay back unless I need you."

"Shayna..." Pierce narrowed his eyes.

She gave him a look that allowed no argument, then turned to face the crowd.

Alvar stood next to a man who stood well over six-feet-tall. Behind them were several vampires. "Hello, Queen Shayna. Yes, word does travel fast." He glanced at the umbrella in her hand. "Meet my new friend, Linc. We needed someone else on our side to lead the lesser minions after you captured Radella. I wonder why you haven't killed her."

"What do you want?" Shayna crossed her arms and donned her armor, then dropped down to his side.

"While you are beautiful and fierce," he said, "your armor doesn't intimidate me, nor does Deema and the three humans wearing theirs. I've armor of my own, should I choose to wear it." He glanced at Agatha. "I see you have a shifter of your own. Impressive size for a dog, but no match for my pet. Show them."

Linc changed to a black panther and bared his fangs.

"Again, I ask you what you want?" Shayna struck the tip of the umbrella against the sidewalk, shooting sparks in every direction.

Alvar jumped back, his gaze widened.

"Afraid of a little bit of the Light?" Shayna grinned and struck harder, emitting a bright aura around herself. With the title of queen came an increase of her powers.

All but Alvar retreated several feet. "You cannot harm me with the Light."

"Oh, but I can." She moved forward. "When you turned traitor, you become weaker against the Light with each passing day. Soon you'll be no better than the foul demon you follow."

He continued backward as she slowly advanced. When a tree blocked him, he waved a hand at Linc. "Show her what you're capable of."

The shifter charged, faster than any animal in the natural kingdom. Shayna snapped her fingers when Agatha started to advance, stopping the witch, and stepped to the side to avoid the shifter.

Linc met dead air, sliding across the pavement. Crouching, he turned to spring again. "You're fast," he purred. "But I'm faster."

"Really?" Shayna shot a blue laser from her hand, freezing the shifter in place. "Your pet kitty is no match for my magic now that I am Queen." She smiled at Alvar. "Would you like to try again?"

"You'll regret ever accepting that staff." He put a hand on the panther's head and teleported them both away.

Shayna turned to the vampires. "Well? Are you staying to fight?"

They shrugged and darted in different directions.

Shayna held up a hand at the civilians watching everything from a few feet away. "Filming a movie, folks. Nothing more than smoke and mirrors." She smiled and led her group back in the building to the sound of applause.

CYNTHIA MELTON

2
Deema

Deema stared at Clark's sleeping face and wondered for the thousandth time what binding herself to him would be like. If she did, a couple hundred of the years she had left in her life would transfer to him. More if he had even a speck of fae blood in him, which he didn't. She fingered the enchanted cross around his neck.

He opened his dark eyes and smiled. "Have I told you how glad I am to have you as my protector?"

She laughed. "Have I told you how glad I am that you have no deceit or malice in your heart as Marshal does? That is why you have a protector, my sweet."

"It wasn't always that way. And Marshal isn't deceitful, just jealous." He kissed her and rolled out of bed. "Not until Shayna arrived and showed me the power of the Light did I lose a lot of my fear. I am truly thankful you came back to our side."

"No more so than I." She rolled to her back and stared at the ceiling. Having followed the dark for so long, nothing felt better than returning where she belonged. She'd almost waited too long and would have been trapped as one of Kasdeya's minions for eternity.

"I must attend The Glen with Shayna part of today," she called to Clark in the bathroom.

"I'll be at the station when you return." He exited, tying a tie around his neck. "If Marshal and I go on a call, I'll make sure he's wearing the cross and that Agatha goes with us."

Deema laughed, throwing aside the bed sheet. "Good luck with that. She's infatuated with television."

"She'll go if Shayna requests it. I'll ask for that first thing." He bent down and gave her a lingering kiss that sent her pulse racing. "You make me wish I had fae blood."

She almost said so did she, but only smiled. Until she knew whether she wanted to make a lifetime commitment, it was better she not give him false hope.

Once she escorted Clark safely to the precinct, she joined Shayna in her throne room. "My queen." She bowed. "How is Queen Linette?"

"Improving slowly. Get up, Deema, it's embarrassing to have you grovel over a mere fae such as myself." Shayna frowned. "Queen Linette leaves tomorrow with a nurse to wherever she deems it imperative to go and risk her health. Are you ready to stand and listen with me as faeries make their requests?"

"Sounds fun." Deema shuddered, taking her place to the left and slightly behind Shayna's throne. She couldn't think of anything more boring. "There is something I'd like to discuss when we're finished."

"Of course." Shayna's features smoothed into an impassive mask as the throne room doors opened.

Earin strolled in, head high, back straight, and bowed. "My queen."

"Arise and state your request."

His lifted his gaze. "Our newest group of warriors is ready for a test. I'd like to take a small group of them into the human world to test them against the vampires and demons they'll encounter in a battle."

Shayna thought for a moment. "Only Deema and I have been fighting them. Having too many of us there will raise suspicion among the humans."

"In all due respect, your highness," his tone didn't sound respectful to Deema's ears, "that was before the enemy knew of our numbers. There is no reason to hide our strength now. Alvar has told them all they need to know."

"Watch your tone," Deema warned, clenching her fists.

Shayna raised her hand. "It's fine." She leaned forward. "Are you sure, Earin? What if we lose some of our young warriors?"

"On the battlefield, we had only our seasoned fighters. We cannot fight again with those who are inexperienced. They need this." His eyes flashed.

"Are they fully equipped with armor and weapons?"

He nodded.

"Very well. I put them in your capable hands." When he made no move to leave, she asked, "something more?"

His gaze flicked to Deema. "In private, please?"

"Insolence." Deema stormed through an archway and headed to the infirmary to say goodbye to Queen Linette. She could never think of the former ruler as anything but queen. In her heart, there were two rulers until Queen Linette returned to her throne.

The queen sat up in bed, fully dressed, a plate of food on a tray in front of her. "Hello, Deema. How are you enjoying your new role as advisor to Shayna?"

"Advisor? I thought I was there to provide support and watch her back."

The queen frowned. "You're there for anything she requires. Is there something wrong?"

"I fear Earin doesn't respect Shayna's new position and may cause trouble for her with the other faeries."

She smiled. "I believe Shayna can handle her own with him and his tender ego."

Deema took a deep breath. "There is something I would ask you, but now that you are no longer ruling, I fear it might not be appropriate."

"You are most likely right. Shayna is your counsel now." She set down her fork. "I know of what you will ask. You question binding yourself to a human."

"Yes."

"Talk to Shayna. She knows the rules and has the same questions. I'm sure the two of you will do what is right."

Shayna

"Speak, Earin. There are others who seek my attention." Shayna breathed deeply through her nose. She was a warrior, not someone content to sit and listen to the problems of others, nor did she enjoy verbal conflict. She enjoyed the feel of a sword in her hand more than a staff.

He knelt, his gaze locked with hers. "You need a king to help you rule. I ask you again to bind yourself to me."

"You ask me this time for the power it would afford you. The queen is not allowed to bind to anyone—fae or human."

"You have the power to change the law. I have always loved you, Shayna." He put a hand over his heart. "Why do you not believe me?"

She sighed. "Find another, Earin. My heart belongs to Pierce."

"A mixed-blood. One you cannot have while you reign as queen." His lip curled. "You waste your time."

"We are finished. Guards, escort him out."

Earin shot her a hard gaze and marched from the room before he could be escorted out, leaving Shayna wearied. Each time they came in contact with each other, he made the same demand. She could never bind to such an arrogant fool, even if she didn't love another.

Faerie after faerie came in with requests as legitimate as a squabble with a neighbor to ridiculous as the variety of vegetables available in the garden. By the time the last faerie left, exhaustion weighed on her shoulders. How had Queen Linette bore it all? She stood and made her way to the queen's chambers where Deema would meet her.

Her trusted friend arrived seconds after Shayna. "Thank the Light, a true friend." Shayna pushed open the double doors and stepped into a crystal cathedral of a room. A rainbow of light shimmered in the crystal walls and across the surface of the marble floor. Shayna draped the white silk cloak she wore over the back of a chair with carved figures of flower, butterflies, and cherubs in the polished wood.

"I think some of those who visited came only out of curiosity to see how I would handle their silly requests." She fell back across the bed and sank into the thick feather mattress. "I'm anxious to hear what you want to talk about."

"If you're tired, it can wait."

Shayna sat up. "I'm never too tired to talk to you. Let's talk as friends and not queen and one of her subjects, please."

Deema twisted the hem of her lavender gown. "Why have you not bound yourself to Pierce?" She lifted her gaze. "I know you care for him."

"More than anything," Shayna whispered. "I fully intended to before becoming queen. Now, my responsibilities will keep us apart, and the law forbids a fae to marry anyone while in a position of leadership."

"A temporary problem. Queen Linette will someday return."

She nodded and narrowed her eyes. "Why do you ask?"

"I'm thinking of making the commitment to Clark."

"A full-blooded human? It will shorten your life by hundreds of years, Deema."

"If I should choose to bind, I would gladly give up some of my life to extend his. Besides, if we reside here, rather than his world, it won't shorten much."

"Yet, you are uncertain. Why?"

Deema paced in front of the bed. "It's an enormous decision. I've only recently returned to the Light, but having worked and fought alongside this man…I've fallen in love with his gentle spirit." She stopped and locked a shimmering gaze on Shayna. "Am I wrong?"

Shayna swallowed back tears. "No."

"Do I have your blessing?" She folded her hands in front of her.

"It is not mine to give." Shayna sat up and grasped her friend's hands. "I know I'm the queen, but I can't get the stars to line up for my own traitorous heart, much less someone else's." What she wouldn't give for the freedom to say yes to Pierce. To spend the rest of her life with him. She, too, would have to give up some of her years, but not as many as Deema due to Pierce's leprechaun blood. "All I can advise is for you to think hard about the decision. There is no turning back once the physical deed is done."

"I know."

"Then, that's settled." Shayna grinned. "We are both heartbroken fools. Shall we go join the men who have caused us this wonderful distress?"

The sounds of battle met them the moment they stepped through the portal. Unsheathing her sword, Shayna dashed into the center of the fray and cut the head from a vampire about to sink its weapon into the back of one of the young fae warriors. Oh, it felt good to swing her sword rather than wag her tongue. She flashed a grin at Deema, then plunged the sword into the headless chest, turning it to ash.

Earin gave a war cry and threw a dagger. He missed, the knife imbedding into the trunk of an oak tree. Before the vampire could charge again, he tossed another, this time hitting his target.

Three unskilled faerie warriors fought with no style or discipline, hacking at their foe and stumbling under the weight of their swords.

"Focus," Shayna ordered. "See your target. Know where he is at all times. Then you attack. Backs together, weapons ready." She shot Earin a cold glance. "Words when this is through." She parried another attack.

Soon five vampires, now turned to dust, floated away on the breeze.

"We had it under control," Earin said, sheathing his sword.

"It did not appear that way." She clenched her jaw. "Get these battered warriors to the infirmary and step up their training before bringing them out here again or you'll spend time in the kitchen."

"Yes, my queen." His words dripped sarcasm.

"You will have to discipline him at some point," Deema said, "or his disrespect will worsen."

"I know." Shayna took a deep breath and teleported, never wanting to have to follow through with disciplining the faerie she had almost committed to. There were more unpleasant duties to being queen than there were pleasant.

Pierce

Going stir-crazy, Pierce grabbed his jacket and weapon and stormed from the precinct to join his partners on a domestic dispute. The same address as the day before when the wife had refused to press charges. Enough was enough.

"What do we have?" he asked, meeting Payson and Marshal outside the apartment building.

"Three rather large demons entered through the

fourth-floor window." Marshal pointed up. "If we don't do something, I have no doubt the husband will kill his wife and child."

"Neither do I. Necklaces on? Weapons ready?" When both men nodded, Pierce led the way into the building, hoping they could take the demons on their own. How large was large?

"We need the women," Marshal said. "We haven't fought demons this size before. I swear they were at least the size of men."

"I know, but with Shayna being queen, they're sometimes needed elsewhere. We can do this." Pierce hoped, anyway.

They climbed the stairs to the stench of urine and vomit. Their shoes slapped on concrete steps littered with garbage and dirty diapers. Upon reaching the fourth floor, Pierce held a finger to his lips and pressed his ear to the door of apartment 412.

Loud voices greeted him. A child wailed. A woman pleaded.

Pierce almost jumped out of his skin when Shayna and Deema appeared on the floor landing in an array of blue and purple sparks. "I'm glad to see you two, but you almost gave me a heart attack. We have at least three humans and the same number of rather large demons inside. The man is threatening to shoot himself and his family."

"Then, let's stop him." Shayna knocked on the door. "Police. Open up."

"No," a voice hissed as the twisted features of a demon slid through the wood of the door. "This man is ours."

"I don't think so." Shayna shoved the demon out of sight.

Pierce stepped back and placed a hard kick on the door, breaking the lock, then stepped aside so Shayna and Deema could enter first. Following close behind, he pulled his vial of holy water from his pocket.

Two demons were perched on the back of a faded sofa where a sobbing woman and a screaming toddler sat. The third had a hand on the shoulder of a man with his finger on the trigger of a pistol.

"One more step and I shoot." The man aimed at the woman. "First her, then the child, then myself."

"Save us the trouble and shoot yourself first, dude." Marshal edged around the room, putting himself between the woman and child.

Falling into the familiar routine of good cop, bad cop, Pierce held up a hand. "That's enough, detective. Sir, we're here to help you."

"Be gone," Shayna ordered. "Or fight and be destroyed."

The man's eyes widened. "You can't talk to me that way."

"Not you," Pierce said, grinning. "The demon behind you."

"What?" The man glanced over his shoulder. That's all Pierce needed in order to rush forward and tackle him to the floor. Payson stepped on the man's wrist and removed the weapon.

"Ma'am." Marshal motioned for the door. "Please take the child and go. We won't harm your husband."

She raced away.

Pierce cuffed the man, then stood with the others to face the demons. He glanced at Shayna and grinned, "This is how I like it. You and me fighting side by side."

3
Deema

Once the woman and child were out of the room and the door secured with holy water to keep the evil inside the room, the three demons surrounded the armed man. Deema grasped the hilt of her sword with both hands and advanced.

The human man shrieked and fell to his knees, putting his cuffed hands over his head. "Please, don't. kill. me." Unable to see what tormented him, he feared Deema instead.

Deema snarled. He hadn't cared about his wife's pleas. She motioned her head for Payson to drag the man away as Shayna stepped to her side. Marshal and Pierce put their backs to the faeries as the demons surrounded them.

"You cannot win this war," one said.

"We've heard that before." Deema cut a glance at Shayna. "When did they learn to speak?"

She shrugged. "I'm sure there are more tricks in Abaddon's pocket."

"You dare to speak his name?" The demon growled and sprang.

Deema jumped in front of Shayna. The demon's clawed hand raked at her arm. Blood welled and dripped on the black and white linoleum. Deema fell as fire burned through the wound. Never had she experienced such pain.

Payson cried her name as he dashed forward and flung what was left of his holy water into the demon's face. The creature howled with pain and slid down the wall, disappearing in a cloud of inky smoke.

"Get back, Payson." Deema's heart leaped into her throat as the other two demons converged on the man she loved.

"You three, get out of here, Pierce." Shayna whirled, shoving herself between the demons and Payson. The demons immediately surrounded her. Shayna gasped and staggered to the side.

Deema struggled to her feet, blood running down her arm. They wanted Shayna, the queen. Deema mustn't let that happen.

"No." Payson fought his way to her side. "Together we fight or together we leave."

"Protect Shayna," Deema said. "It's her they want."

With a war cry, Pierce lunged forward and shoved Shayna to the side. "You cannot have her."

The remaining two demons slashed and whirled like two six-foot tornadoes in the apartment. Furniture shattered, lamps busted, and still the battle raged. Deema's hands slipped on her sword as the blood continued to pour from her wound. Where had these demons received their strength?

The three detectives and two faeries formed a tight circle, backs together. Deema fought past the pain and encroaching weakness, trying to keep one eye on her foe and the other on her queen. She failed as Shayna fell.

Earin appeared behind the demons and sliced the head from one before turning to the other. Deema had never been so grateful to see the insolent fool.

The demons were destroyed.

Deema leaned heavily on her sword. "How did you know we were in trouble?"

"Shayna called me." He rushed to the queen's side and shoved Pierce out of the way. "She's wounded, as are you. We must get back to The Glen."

It was too soon after the vampire bite for Shayna to enter into such a fierce confrontation. Tears welling in Deema's eyes blurred at the sight of her bloody queen slumped against the wall.

Pierce

"I'll take her." Pierce scooped Shayna into his

arms. "Teleport us. All of us."

Earin scowled but put one hand on his shoulder and grasped Deema's hand with the other. As she gripped the hands of the other two, he took them to The Glen.

Upon entering the portal, Earin moved his hand from Pierce as if his skin burned. Without looking back, he headed toward the infirmary ahead of them.

"Shayna." Pierce peered into her face.

Her eyelids fluttered, then opened. "Put me down."

"You're hurt."

"Look at the faces of my people. They are frightened. They need to know my injuries aren't fatal, and they still have someone to rule them."

He glanced at the wide-eyed, pale faces of The Glen's inhabitants. With a sigh, he lowered her to her feet but kept one arm firmly around her waist.

Once they reached the infirmary, Shayna and Deema were immediately placed on well-padded cots covered with clean, white linen bedding. The nurse cast a wary eye at the humans and hesitated to offer her services.

"They fought for us, Nurse Zina." Shayna sent the woman a stern glance. "You will care for them as you do us."

The nurse nodded and waved a younger faerie close. The younger woman applied salve to the men's cuts and scrapes while Zina tended to Shayna. "You were lucky, my queen. Superficial and easily healed."

"I'm glad to hear it. It burns like fire and bled

heavily."

"As a scratch from one of hell's creatures does." She glanced at Deema. "Your guard didn't fare as well and will require stitches."

"If she is more wounded than I, then why did I fall, unable to get to my feet?"

"Because you aren't ready to fight, my queen. Not a long battle anyway. You are still recovering from the bite." She handed Shayna, then Pierce a cup of vile-smelling tea. "Both of you, drink. You'll feel better in a few minutes." She turned to care for Deema.

Pierce perched on the side of Shayna's hospital bed. "Don't shove me out of the way again."

"Don't step in front of me, and I won't have to." She smiled, then grimaced as she sipped the tea. "Nasty stuff."

He entwined his fingers with hers. "I want to take care of you to the best of my ability. I know I've asked this before, but please let me."

"I want to care for you." She scooted to a more upright sitting position. "I'm more powerful, Pierce. When I am recovered, I can fight all day and into the night. Your human body cannot last that long no matter how hard you try."

"Then, we'll care for each other. Just don't push me away again."

Her gaze locked on his. "I'll try."

He traced circles in her palm. "You've never been targeted before. Is it because you are queen?"

"Yes, just as Queen Linette had been during the fight in Wyoming. Taking the queen would put the odds in their favor."

"Then stay out of the fights. Stay here in The Glen where you'll be safe." An ache settled in his heart. He knew the answer to his request before she answered.

"I'm a warrior." She slipped her hand free of his and turned away. "That is what I have always been called to do. I will not stop fighting for the Light to overpower the darkness. Not as long as I draw breath."

Using his forefinger, he turned her to face him. "I understand. You and I are the same, Shayna, but I couldn't bear…" he swallowed against the lump in his throat. "Seeing you lying on the floor, covered in blood, I thought I'd lost you. You may not have committed to me physically, but I am yours. I could never love another." He took her hand again and placed a kiss in the center of her palm. "I give you all that I am."

She gasped. "Pierce, those words uttered here in The Glen can never be taken back."

"Good." He grinned. "Because I will keep saying them until they stick."

Her eyes shimmered. "There can be nothing between us as long as I am queen. It is the law. I cannot bind to anyone."

"Then I'll wait until Queen Linette returns." He leaned over and kissed her lips, lingering just a bit before straightening. "Rest. I'll see you at dinner."

Payson and Marshal followed him out the door where Earin waited in the hall, blocking their way. The faerie glared. "You will never have her. It is me she called when all seemed lost." He thumped his chest.

"If you weren't such a nuisance, she'd have chosen you as a partner a long time ago, and you'd be by her side instead of Deema." Pierce crossed his arms. "It's me she wants now. Me she steps in front of when danger threatens. She only needs your fighting strength."

"You'll be her death," the faerie spit.

Pierce's fear. Still, he'd die before allowing her to perish and no sour faerie could change that.

Earin transferred his attention to the other two. "Your kind isn't welcome here."

"Considering your queen invited us, I'd say we're more than welcome," Marshal said before glancing around. "This is my first visit, and I must say you aren't the most welcoming committee I've ever experienced. Would you mind giving us a tour?" He grinned.

Earin's features hardened. He spun on a booted heel and marched away, his steps echoing along the marble hallway.

"That prissy boy has a stick so far up his—"

"Watch your mouth here," Pierce warned. "Foul language is not welcome. There will be others who feel the same as Earin. We're only human, after all, and few will welcome us as equals."

"Stupid considering how much we risk for their sake as well as our own." He watched a female in a yellow gown stroll by. "I do like the way their women look in their clothes, though. Their skin seems to shimmer through the fabric. Very provocative."

Pierce agreed on both counts, remembering his first sight of Shayna in her native clothing. As for the risk and prejudice…things were as they were and no words would change the facts. "Wait until you taste the food. You'll never want to leave." He smiled and led the way to the dining hall.

Kasdeya

"The stupid faerie queen and her friends disposed of your new creations fast enough." Kasdeya paced the room like a caged lion. She wanted out! He didn't want to risk her safety, Abaddon said. He needed her to lead his followers, he said, so she must stay out of harm's way. She cursed and flung her empty whiskey glass against the wall, showering the plaster with glass and amber liquid.

"Such a temper," Alvar said, studying his nails. "I'll make more. A legion of them, if you wish. You're sure to win in the end if you have enough of my creations."

"Then why are you sitting here?" She sneered into his face. "Get busy!"

With a dramatic sigh, he got to his feet. "As you wish." He snapped his fingers and disappeared.

Where did the faerie go when he left her? She'd asked a multitude of times and he always skirted the question. Did he go to see Abaddon? Would he replace her as the demon leader's right hand? Or did he have a secret place to do his evil business and plans of taking over, known only to him?

Kasdeya plopped onto the black leather sofa. She'd given up her mortal life for one of power and eternity. If she were cast aside, she'd be doomed, returned to the human world again and despised. She would use the faerie for all she could, then have him eliminated. She didn't need the competition. Her entire future stemmed on her remaining in control and ridding the faerie of a queen.

CYNTHIA MELTON

4
Deema

Deema lifted her sword, testing the weight against the pull of the stitches in her arm. The burning from the demon's claws had subsided almost immediately after the nurse applied the salve. It could have been worse. Shayna could have been killed or taken. Without a queen with enough strength to lead, the fae would fall. Darkness would cover everything. It was Deema's job not to let that happen.

"No, it isn't." Shayna sat up, swinging her legs over the side of the bed. "It's mine as the queen."

"You can't go out there anymore." Deema lowered her sword. She hadn't been aware she'd spoken out loud.

"I can, and I will. I won't argue with you, too." Shayna stood and draped her cloak around her shoulders. "It's time for dinner. Fight by my side, but you will not fight without me." Head high, she strolled out of the infirmary.

Deema had no choice but to follow. Without glancing at Shayna's stony face, she took the seat to the other woman's right and sat. Pierce sat to Shayna's left, Marshal next to him, leaving Payson to sit next to Deema.

"What's wrong?" he whispered.

"I'll explain later." She shook her head. "Not here."

Shayna shot them a quick glance, then motioned for them to sit. "Before we eat, I have something I need to say." After she had their attention, she continued, "I am queen, yes, but I am still Shayna, Warrior of the Light. There will be no more argument about what any of you think my role should be. I will not shirk my duties here, nor will I lay down my sword. Subject closed." She picked up a gold-plated fork and started to eat.

Deema stifled a sigh and dug into a pile of bright yellow vegetables, keeping one eye on Shayna in case she needed her assistance, and another on Payson and Marshal who had yet to sample The Glen's delicacies.

She wasn't disappointed. At their first taste, eyes widened, and groans of pleasure left their lips. Human food would never taste the same to them after today. She chuckled.

"I never want to leave." Payson patted his stomach and sat back. "How can you not be as big as a horse?"

"Our food gives us only the nourishment we need, nothing more." She smiled at the pleasure on his face. If the final outcome landed on the side of the Light, he might get his wish at staying.

When they'd finished, Shayna stood. "I request the presence of all of you in my chambers. Now. That includes you, Earin." She strode away, her cloak billowing out behind her.

Deema shrugged when they all looked at her and stood. "The queen has spoken, people, and I don't think she's happy with us."

It was a subdued group that entered the queen's chambers. She must have asked someone ahead of time because enough chairs had been brought in to seat them all. Two silent guards stood outside the door, one of them pushing the door open as they approached.

"Sit." Shayna sat on a chair placed in front of those in a semi-circle. "Do not say anything until I have finished speaking." She set her staff against the wall. "I will speak as your ruler, then you will speak to me as my friends. I value your opinions."

Deema opened her mouth to speak, then snapped it closed at a stern glare from Shayna. Rather than risk the queen's wrath, she sat.

Payson took her hand and whispered, "Don't worry. You're her best friend."

Right, but she was also beneath Shayna's current station in life. Friend or not, she could be removed of her position as the queen's advisor. She gave his hand a squeeze, then folded her hands in her lap.

Shayna

The others looked so worried. It grieved Shayna to see them so bothered, but there were things that needed setting straight, and she couldn't wait another minute.

"I began my warrior training as soon as I could hold a sword. It didn't take long for the masters to see my potential." She locked gazes with Pierce's loving one and drew strength from the warmth she saw there. "Since that time, I've never wanted to be anything but a warrior. I did not choose the position of queen, yet here I am, for a time at least.

"On that mountaintop, Queen Linette was injured in a vain attempt from the other side to capture her. We have discovered forces are darker and more powerful than we thought. Today, the same thing almost happened to me, but my fellow fighters stopped that from happening. I do hope you caught the *fellow fighters* statement, because that is what we are. Queen Linette didn't shirk her duty of leading her people in a battle despite the possible danger, and neither will I." Her gaze shifted to Earin.

"You have been a faithful follower of the Light for centuries, Earin, yet you've invited a seed of jealousy into your heart. The Light cannot continue to live where such a thing exists. These men," she waved a hand at the detectives, "risk as much or more than we do. They don't have the powers we do, nor the strength, yet they take up their weapons and fight alongside us because they know it must be done. Earin, my fellow warrior, I will not tolerate your dislike for them anymore. Pledge your loyalty or leave The Glen. Those are your only choices."

Earin stood, his face impassive. For several seconds he met her stare, then knelt, his head bowed. "I pledge my loyalty, my life, and my sword, my queen."

"Then rise, my friend, and we will speak no more of this." She placed a hand on his head. "I am pleased at your choice as your strength is greatly needed. Now, leave us, please, as you have important work to do."

He nodded and left without glancing at the others.

Shayna released a long breath, some of the tension leaving her body. She'd almost feared he would leave The Glen. When the door closed behind him, she smiled at the others. "Any questions?"

"No questions, just a statement," Pierce said, his eyes red. "I realize we can do nothing to stop you from going out there, so I'll say this." He moved to his knees in front of her and took her hands in his. "I will always put myself between you and danger. I am not one of your subjects, but I am the man who loves you. If you cannot allow that, then you'll have to send me away."

"The same goes for me." Deema knelt.

Payson and Marshal followed, saying in unison, "me too."

Tears poured down Shayna's face. Those she cared about more than anything in any world would die for her and her for them. "Stand, please," she forced out, forming a circle. "I pledge to you right now that I accept your love and offer of protection as warriors side-by-side, not queen and subjects."

"Agreed," Pierce said, wrapping her into a hug. "Let's go kick some demon butt. I'm sure Agatha is going stir-crazy, and I have a station to run. Are you and Deema well enough to return to our world?"

"Yes." Deema waved her sword. "Just a little stiff. Nothing that can't be worked out. Besides, I've salve in my pocket to keep the stitches soft. I say it's time to go and devise a plan against this new species of demon."

Shayna agreed. "We need to talk to the oldest in our group. Agatha may know more than we." They trooped to the portal, then teleported to Shayna's hotel room.

"Have you considered buying a condo?" Marshal plopped into a chair. "It's got to be expensive renting this place day after day."

"No, but I'll consider such a thing." Shayna set her staff on the bed. "Agatha, we need your wisdom."

"Finally, someone with a brain." Agatha turned off the television. "I'm sitting here growing bored since your highness forbade me to leave this room."

"I didn't forbid anything." Shayna sat in a navy-blue chair. "I suggested it in order to keep Kasdeya from knowing we have a witch on our side."

"Whatever." Agatha grinned. "Need me to bite someone?"

Shayna laughed. "No, but we did encounter some very strong demons with poisonous claws and the ability to speak."

Agatha's cheeky grin faded. "You don't say?" She tapped a finger on her chin. "Now, be quiet and let me think." After several minutes, she said, "I need to leave for a while. I'll be back by dark." She transformed into a butterfly.

Marshal opened the door to let her out. "She's a strange one."

"I don't like her leaving. What if something happens to her?" Shayna moved to the window and watched the blue-and-black speck until it grew too small. The oldest living creature in either world, the witch had the heart of a warrior and harbored no fear in her heart.

Still her leaving was dangerous. She could be caught or killed. A butterfly might be a good disguise, but there were people out there who killed insects with no thought it might be anything else.

Pierce joined her, putting an arm around her shoulder. "She hasn't lived this long by being stupid. Agatha will be fine."

She rested her head on his shoulder. "I know. Keep the faith."

By nightfall every nerve in Shayna's body was strung as tight as violin strings. She watched as Deema applied salve to her stitches. Payson held the jar for her. Marshal flicked through the television channels. Pierce lay on the bed, his arm over his eyes.

Shayna turned back to the window. "Open the door. She's coming." She smiled as the blue-and-black butterfly approached the building. "Marshal, go make sure she gets in the building and on the elevator without harm."

He nodded and darted out the door. Minutes later, he returned, his hand gently cradling Agatha. He placed her on a chair as she turned back into herself.

"Well, that was an ordeal." The witch smoothed her robes. "Kasdeya is a naughty girl." She grinned. "She has that faerie traitor turning regular demons into monsters. Not that they weren't already, but now they are a hundred times worse. I hovered outside her window for hours and watched her pace. Something has that demon woman anxious. I don't think there is any love lost between her and Alvar, either. If looks could kill…"

"You couldn't find out what's bothering her?" Shayna sat on the edge of the bed.

"No, once Alvar arrived, told her the creations were being worked on, then left, she paced and drank and paced some more. My guess is she's not happy with Alvar, Abaddon, or both."

Good news, but what to do with the information?

5
Deema

Deema escorted Shayna to the dungeon below the throne room. Radella, bound with silver chains bolted to the marble wall, sneered, "Come to grace me with your presence? I'm honored." Her eyes widened. "Even more so to know I'm in the presence of a queen." She spit at their feet. "Did I manage to kill Linette?"

"Not even close." Deema gripped the silver-tipped dagger on her belt. "Do not speak unless asked."

"I don't follow your rules, faerie." Radella flashed her fangs, then turned to Shayna. "I see my love bite didn't cause you any lasting harm."

Shayna remained impassive. "We've some questions to ask. If you don't answer willingly, I'm sure Deema can help convince you. What is the poison you used on the knife that cut our queen?"

Radella sneered, "Something you can't figure out." She raised her eyebrows. "Fancy that. Bring me some blood of a faerie and I'll answer your questions."

"You'll answer them or suffer." Deema held the tip of her knife to the vampire's throat. "One little nick. Please, Shayna."

"Not yet. Answer the question, Radella."

"I don't know. Kasdeya gave us the knives. Now my turn. How did you survive my bite?"

"Through the painful task of having my blood cleansed." Shayna smiled. "There is not a drop of your saliva anywhere in my veins."

"Pity." Radella heaved a sigh. "Do you intend to starve me to death?"

"You won't die." Deema laughed. "You can only die once, undead spawn. Feeding only makes you powerful, and we can't have that, can we?"

"You'll be the first I kill when I escape these chains."

"Oooh, I'm frightened." Deema gave an exaggerated shudder.

"Stop your squabbling." Shayna pulled up a carved stool and sat. "Were you aware Alvar is creating a new type of demon? Ones with poison on their claws and the capability of speech? Where is he doing this?"

"Yay for the other side."

Deema made a tiny prick in the vampire's skin with the knife.

Radella screamed in pain and cursed.

"Answer the question." Shayna motioned for Deema to step back.

"I didn't know faeries were capable of vile acts." Radella tried to put a hand to her neck, only to have the chains stop her. "If I was aware of the new demons, I would have had them at the battle. I have no idea where Alvar goes."

"He has a shifter named Linc at his side. Ring any bells?" Deema sheathed her knife.

"Big guy? Yeah, I hired him right before I torched the club. I would've turned him if he weren't already fae." She laughed. "So, Alvar found him. Good. He'll be a worthy foe for you. I hope he bites your head off."

Shayna stood and strolled away, not glancing back. Deema flashed a grin at the bound vampire and hurried to catch up.

"We learned nothing," Shayna said. "I spent time in her company for naught, relieving her boredom and provided nothing more than entertainment."

"We need to follow Alvar the next time he leaves Kasdeya. I can shrink and—"

"Do you not remember getting captured the last time?"

"Send Earin."

"He's needed elsewhere."

"I can train the new warriors as well as he. Maybe better."

Shayna stopped and faced her. "You're needed with me here and in the human world. I'll think of something." Rather than head to her room, Shayna continued to the portal, changing into her human clothes as they passed through.

Deema held her questions until they were in the

hotel. "We've come early today."

Before answering, Shayna shoved the curtains aside and stared out the window.

Deema shrugged at Agatha's curious look, then joined the other faerie at the window. "What's wrong?"

"What do you see?"

"The day is like dusk."

"Yes, and it is nearly noon. Time is running out. The darkness thickens."

"What do you want to do?" Agatha asked.

"Find out where Alvar is making his creatures."

Shayna

"Can you help, Agatha?" Shayna turned from the window.

"Hold on." The witch dug in her bag and pulled out a crystal ball. "These aren't always accurate when I'm using it in a room covered with a magic shield, but let's see what we can see."

She peered over the witch's shoulder until Agatha delivered an elbow to her stomach. "Very well," Shayna said.

She returned to stare out the window in hopes of catching sight of…something. Peering through a veil of magic allowed her to see those who were not human. The demons were an inky black, the vampires gray, the shape-shifters brown, the leprechauns, green…She'd not caught a glimpse of the red that was Kasdeya in days. Nor could she spot the silver haze of Alvar which would turn to a dark shade of metal the longer he followed the dark. A shadow of unease settled around Shayna.

"I've got something," Agatha called.

Shayna rushed to the table where the ball sat and peered inside. "That's The Glen. No, impossible. There are no mountains. Where is a place like this in our world?"

"I haven't been there since I was a child," Deema said, "but I think that's the Circle of Mushrooms where my mother's people reside. I was told the dark-haired faeries had virtually disappeared. Even trade had stopped between them and Linette's followers." Her eyes widened. "Do you think they've been recruited to the other side?"

"I hope not." Shayna fell into a chair. "We need to find this place and speak to their queen." If the dark-hairs joined with Kasdeya, all would be lost. Gorna would know where to find the place. "I need to visit the dragons."

"I'll go with you. I wantto see if I can salvage my relationship with Dragona." Deema looked anything but eager. Since her time of following the dark, the dragon whose scales made up her armor had turned her back on the faerie.

"I need to go with you." Agatha replaced the ball in the bag. "I'm running short of herbs that can only be found in the dragon's valley."

"They'll let you in?" Surprise shot through

Shayna.

"Of course, they will. What? You think they have something against witches?" She scowled.

"Yes."

"They only deny those who practice black magic and none of them are left in any world." She slung her bag over her shoulder. "Let's go. Time is wasting."

Once back in The Glen, Shayna summoned her winged horse, Crystal. Two servants hurried forward with a sled. "Since there are three of us, we can't ride on her back."

The other two climbed inside after Shayna. With a flick of the reins, Crystal soared into the air toward the dragon's valley, stopping in front of a steep mountain. Shayna jumped down and patted the horse's snout. "Wait for us here. We'll return in a few hours, for the walk before us is long."

"I hate walking." Agatha stomped her foot. "Can't you teleport us there?"

"If I could, I would. This is one place my magic is no good." Shayna stepped through a crack in the side of the mountain, leaving the others to follow or not. Agatha grumbled the entire hike until Shayna wanted to strangle the witch. The green valley of the dragons had never seemed so inviting.

"I'm off. I'll meet you here in an hour." Agatha slugged away in search of her herbs.

The ground shook as Gorna landed in front of them. "Queen Shayna."

Shayna smiled. "My friend." She leaned against the dragon's neck. "I've come with a request. Do you know the way to the Circle of Mushrooms?"

"I do." She cast a yellow-eyed gaze at Deema. "I see you've returned. Is this some kind of trickery?"

Deema shook her head. "I have returned with no deceit in me. Where might I find Dragona?"

"You need only to summon her. She'll either come or she won't." Gorna blew a spark from her nostril.

"Be nice." Shayna patted the dragon's neck. "We'll wait here while Deema makes her request."

Deema

Deema's legs trembled as she moved away from the others and made the telepathic connection with the dragon. Then, she sat on a boulder to wait.

An hour passed. Deema had almost given up hope before the lavender-colored dragon swooped down. Deema bowed. "I beg your forgiveness a thousand times over."

Although not as large as Gorna, Dragona was still impressive with scales that glittered in the light and dark-blue eyes. "You deserted me."

"I was under the delusion the other side would grant me all of my wishes. They strongly influenced me, but I couldn't have been more wrong. I was stupid." Tears welled in her eyes and stung her throat. "I've missed you, my friend."

Dragona looked to where Gorna and Shayna watched. "You work for the queen now?"

"I do. I passed the test and have come back to the Light."

"Then I accept your rejoining. What will you ask of me?"

"We need passage to the Circle of Mushrooms."

"No one has spoken of the place in centuries. The witch will not be welcomed."

"She'll remain here gathering herbs until we return."

"Don't I get a say in the matter?" Agatha crawled from under a bush covered with yellow blossoms. She brushed a leaf from her cloak. "You could be gone for days. I insist upon going. I am on the side of the Light and expect to be treated as such."

"I'll bring her back," Gorna said, "if they refuse her entry."

"I always knew I liked dragons." Agatha smiled. "I've everything I need, so I'm ready."

Two dragons stared, unblinking, until Gorna spoke. "We go when the queen says so."

Shayna laughed and climbed onto the dragon's neck. "You'll get used to her. Come on with me, Agatha. It's best you arrive with the queen."

Deema climbed on Dragona's back. Oh, how she had missed her glittery friend. "Why didn't you fight in the battle?"

"I couldn't fight with you there. Not until we reconciled. Never fear, I will be at the next one. It will be good to fight by your side." With a mighty pump of her wings, they rose into the air.

Agatha held tight to Shayna, her eyes squeezed shut, clearly not as brave with the dragons as she liked to put on. Deema laughed at the sight of Agatha, then nudged gently with her knees. Dragona soared higher, slicing through the clouds. Deema held her arms wide. The wind blew her hair back from her face. She closed her eyes and let the tears fall. She truly was home.

6
Shayna

Shayna directed Gorna to stop outside the crystal walls of the dark-hairs' palace. With Deema and Agatha following her, she clutched her staff in sweaty palms and entered through the gate. As far as she knew, the two halves of the faerie world rarely interacted. Only a few, like Deema, had come under the rule of Linette.

Dark-haired faeries bowed as they passed. Two guards approached along the cobblestoned path, their faces impassive. "Follow us," one of them said, shooting a wary glance at Agatha. "You've been expected."

Shayna's eyes widened. Who expected them and why? Trying not to let her surprise show on her face, she lifted her chin and followed the guards.

They were led to a palace constructed of black glass, so different from the crystal palace she called home that Shayna marveled at the smoothness of its glass-like walls. She wanted to trail her fingers along the surfaces, but kept one holding her staff and the other at her side as befitted a queen.

The guards pushed open a set of double doors at the end of a long hallway, then stepped back to let Shayna and the others enter. At the far side of the room sat a dark-haired queen and a light-haired one.

"Linette!" Shayna knelt at the feet of her queen.

"A queen bows for no one, my friend." Linette motioned her to rise. "Did the witch lead you here?"

"The dragons, although Agatha played a part in its discovery. You're the last one I expected to see here." Shayna turned to the other queen. "Your majesty, it's an honor."

Queen Brigette nodded. "We have much to discuss. Come into my chambers. Leave the others here."

Shayna mouthed, "Sorry" to Deema and Agatha and followed the faerie women through a carved wooden door. Where Linette's chambers were white, Brigette's were done in shades of dark blue and purple.

"Please." Brigette motioned toward two velvet chairs. "I know you must have many questions, Shayna." She smiled. "We will answer all that we can."

Shayna nodded and glanced at Linette. "I didn't know the location of this place until Agatha showed me in her crystal ball. It's a surprise to see you."

"This is where the purest silver can be found," Linette said. "This is where the chains that once bound Abaddon were forged and are forged here again."

Brigette leaned forward. "Why are you here, Shayna? What's this about a crystal ball?"

"Alvar is creating demons that are stronger and bigger than any we've ever seen. They have poisoned claws and the ability to speak. After some searching his whereabouts, Agatha's ball showed he is creating these monsters in your lands." She narrowed her eyes to gauge the other queen's reaction.

Confusion and surprise flitted across her face. "How is that possible without my knowledge?" She glanced at Linette.

"It has to be an enchantment," Linette said. "Alvar is our most powerful in the ways of magic. This wouldn't be out of his ability. Where do you have an area large enough and secluded enough for this to happen?"

So, Linette believed the dark faerie truly wasn't aware of what went on in her lands. Shayna trusted her queen and would also trust the other. "Why were you not at the battle? The darkness will destroy you as well as us."

High spots of color brightened Brigette's cheeks. Her dark eyes flashed. "It wasn't our war to fight. Not then. It appears things may have changed and the war has been brought to us."

"Your un-involvement may be why Alvar chose your lands for his nefarious deeds." Shayna rested her staff across her lap and crossed her arms.

Linette put a calming hand on her shoulder. "We're on one team, here. No judgment or accusations."

"I need to speak with my advisor." Brigette

pressed a button on the arm of her chair.

Seconds later the doors opened, and a dark-haired man entered. "My queen."

Brigette explained Shayna's reason for being there. "Do you know of such a place?"

"I may, but I'd rather not say without proof. Shall I send a scout?"

She nodded. "Make haste. I fear this traitor will attack our lands before moving back to the human world."

"Why would you think so?" Shayna stiffened.

"We've had a few of our warriors disappear on hunting expeditions. It's possible Alvar captured them to train his demons. We've stopped sending anyone outside of our gates because of this." A worry line marred her smooth skin. "We're not getting the training we need because of the danger."

"Come to The Glen," Linette said. "Together we will be unstoppable. Alvar wouldn't dare attack us there. You're too exposed on these plains. You need the protection of our mountains."

"I will think on the matter." She stood. "Come. I'll show you where the chains are being forged. Another reason for my reluctance to leave. It is imperative we finish before going anywhere."

"Bring everyone, my sister-queen." Linette stood and took her hands in hers. "Down to the last child. Let us no longer be separated, but instead, form a world the darkness cannot penetrate."

"Your words sound sweet to my ears. I'll consult my advisor when the scout returns." She sailed out the door, leading them down a flight of stone steps to the floor below.

Shayna motioned for Deema and Agatha to follow. When Brigette raised her brows, she shrugged. "You may need Agatha's insight. I'm beginning to think not even Alvar's magic can rival hers."

Shayna could see the reasoning of the two groups joining together again. Centuries ago the light and dark faeries had divided over an egotistical prince refusing to choose between two sisters and pitted them against each other. To come together again would be the most wonderful thing to happen in many lifetimes.

A furnace burned bright in the stone room below making the place uncomfortably warm. The ringing of an anvil pierced the air. A shining length of silver chain, its links as thick as Shayna's wrist, hung across the room.

"Almost finished, my queen." A large faerie bowed. "All that is needed will be Abaddon."

"We will capture him again." Brigette turned to Agatha. "Show your worth, witch. What can you do to these chains that we cannot? Shayna thinks you are valuable. Prove it."

"I've nothing to prove to a snooty faerie such as yourself, but since my fate is also at stake here, I will help." Agatha gathered her robes around her and approached the chains. For several minutes she stared, sometimes running her fingers over the links. "This is pure. I can infuse it with light. Abaddon will be destroyed this time, not just chained." She glanced at Brigette. "It will take me a few days. I also need a strand of hair from each of you. A strand of three cannot be broken. The fact you are queens who follow the Light is even better." She held out her hand.

"We are not all three queens," Linette said. "I handed over my staff."

"Won't matter. You are still queen in the eyes of many." She wiggled her fingers. "Come on. You're wasting my time, and we have precious little of it."

Deema

Deema watched as two blond strands and one dark were placed in Agatha's palm. She'd never dreamed such a thing was possible in her lifetime. Her mother had told stories of the discontent between the two first sisters. No one thought reconciliation could ever happen.

Hope leaped in her breast. They couldn't lose the fight if they worked together. She glanced at Shayna and grinned.

Shayna returned the smile and came to stand by her side. "This is a miracle."

"You brought this together. You were made to be a queen, Shayna."

"No." She shook her head. "I'll gladly hand the staff back to Linette. She looks well enough now. My place is on the battlefield with you."

"And Pierce." Deema gave her shoulder a

playful bump.

"Of course." Shayna blushed.

"Not to mention, if you are not queen, you can bind to him." A silly law that needed changing. A queen should be able to pass the staff to an offspring upon her passing rather than die childless and hand it over to someone not of her blood.

"I'm aware of that fact." She smiled.

"My queen." A breathless faerie entered and knelt at Brigette's feet. "I've found his lair."

"Rise and tell me."

He brushed his arm across his perspiring forehead. "He is creating an army, my queen. With numbers larger than any I've seen before. These creatures are as tall as I am with long arms and claws that can rip a body to shreds. They've dug into a cave far into the hill beyond the lake. I could see their comings and goings, but I could not penetrate the shield."

Brigette paled. "They will be coming. We will perish. Sound the warning. We must evacuate. Have everyone take only what they can carry and meet in the courtyard. We must teleport out in groups. Non-warriors first." She spun to the men making the chain. "Pack it up. Witch, you stay with them until it is their turn to go."

"Which will be as soon as we're packed, I assume?" Agatha raised a brow.

Brigette nodded.

Agatha pulled a wand from inside her cloak and pointed it at the chain. The chain coiled itself into a crate. "We're ready."

Deema couldn't stop a laugh from escaping.

"My apologies. Agatha is a force to be reckoned with. I'll teleport these folks out and return immediately. Nothing must happen to this crate."

She held hands with the blacksmiths and Agatha. The last man kept one hand firmly on the crate until they landed in the field next to Earin and the training warriors. Deema quickly explained the circumstances.

"I'll come, along with all we can spare." Earin shouted an order for the others to follow, then clasped her hand. They landed in the courtyard of Brigette's castle. "Fascinating place. Dark, yet beautiful."

"Stop gawking and help save these people." Deema hurried to Shayna's side. "I've brought Earin. Each warrior is capable of teleporting with four people."

"Something my people need to work on mastering. We've never needed that particular skill much." Brigette snapped her fingers. "We may not be able to take as many at one time, but I can spare a few who can take two at a time. The rest will be stationed at each gate to guard our evacuation. I must go. We cannot risk losing both queens."

Deema glanced over the approaching crowd, then at the sky growing darker with each passing minute. A frigid breeze ruffled her hair. "They're coming now. I suggest we go at once and not try to stay and fight. We need every warrior we have for the coming future." She kept her gaze locked with Brigette's until the queen saw reason.

Tears shimmered in Brigette's eyes. "We will abandon our home for now." She took the hand of a woman and child and teleported. With each warrior taking the most they could successfully transport, the city was emptied in less than an hour.

Deema left last, making sure all were accounted for. She locked gazes with Alvar who rode on the back of a black steed. Behind him flew a legion of inky creatures. The faerie's scream ricocheted overhead as she snapped her fingers. That was one unhappy faerie.

She landed with laughter still on her lips. "We did it. Just in time, too. Alvar is screaming mad."

"He turned mad the moment he turned traitor." Shayna ordered a multitude of servants to erect tents in a clearing just outside the castle. "Agatha, I need your help in placing a shield no magic can get through. Can you do it?"

"Pshaw. Child's magic." She stalked away muttering how folks still doubted her capabilities.

"The dragons would have left, right? They wouldn't have waited for our return?" Fear rose in Deema's throat.

"I let Gorna know the moment Brigette agreed to leave her palace." Shayna wrapped Deema in a hug. "You'll fall back into the old ways with Dragona in time. Be pleased she took you back."

"I am." She pulled away. "I regret that I didn't give her a thought in my haste to get the faeries to safety."

"You did your job, and quite well. I took care of the rest. Now, my friend, help find these refugees lodging while I plan with Linette and Brigette in my chambers." Head high, Shayna headed for the castle.

By nightfall, all refugees had places to sleep, if only canvas ones. Brigette had a room in the castle along with Linette, who continuously refused to take back the staff. If Shayna's fierce expression at dinner was any indication, her patience ran as thin as the jam on her toast.

While Deema understood her friend's heart, Shayna made an excellent queen. She leaned closer to Linette during dinner. "Pardon my opinion, your majesty, but it would greatly please your best warrior to take back the staff."

Linette's eyes flashed. "You dare advise me?"

Deema shrugged. "You are no longer queen, am I right? If you desire to be treated as such, take back the staff. You seem healed enough, and the chains have been reforged. What are you waiting for? Why force Shayna into a role she doesn't want?"

Sighing, Linette lifted her crystal goblet. "I've quite enjoyed the freedom afforded to those who don't rule. Selfish, I know." She took a sip, then set the goblet back. "I'll take back my place. But…" Her gaze pierced Deema's, "if something should happen to me, I make Shayna my heir. I charge you with the duty of making sure she lives."

"I accept, and I agree wholeheartedly, my queen." Deema glanced at Shayna and winked. Tomorrow, they'd go back to the human world and tell their men of today's happenings. She missed Payson with every beat of her heart and knew Shayna felt the same about Pierce. "You might also consider changing the silly law that says whoever rules must die alone."

"Things are changing," Earin said, tossing his

linen napkin onto his plate. "Witches and humans are saving us, faeries are turning traitor, demons grow bigger. My faith falters."

"Stand firm, warrior. The Light will not be extinguished." Deema stood. "Come. Let me show you something that will lift your heart." She gave a nod to Linette.

Earin scowled but followed her to the clearing.

"We are now two-hundred more warriors strong. We have saved an entire city from certain destruction." She cut him a sideways glance. "By working together with all races, we can accomplish mighty things. The faerie will not win the war alone. We need even the leprechauns and the humans. Probably Agatha most of all."

He stood silent as a small boy chased a runaway ball. The air filled with the sound of laughter. A baby cried and was hushed. "You're right, Deema. The witch will most likely save us all." His mouth quirked. "Oh, the irony."

She chuckled. "You might even learn to like her and the humans, given time, my warrior friend."

His eyes twinkled. "Perhaps. Thank you." He gave a nod and strolled away whistling.

Deema stayed a while longer watching those who resided in the tents. As lanterns were extinguished in preparation for sleep, she turned and headed to her room. Tomorrow would be filled with its own challenges. She looked forward to facing them with her friends.

7
Shayna

Shayna strode straight to Pierce's office and closed the door. A smile played on her lips, she turned slowly and cupped his face in both of her hands before planting a lingering kiss on his lips.

"I'm not complaining, but what's this?" He grinned.

"Linette took the staff back. I can be by your side most of every day."

"I'd take the nights, too, but this is great news." He gave her another kiss. "Sit and tell me where you've been. I've been worried." He resumed his seat behind the desk.

He remained silent while she spoke, the expressions on his face ranging from shock to fear to anger. When she'd finished, he asked, "So, how do we find Abaddon? It can't be easy going up against such evil."

"We've got Agatha trying to locate him. So far none of her tracking spells work." She settled into the chair across from him. "I spoke with Radella, and she didn't know anything about this new breed of demon. Catching Kasdeya might be our first step in locating Abaddon."

"How do you propose doing that? She's well-guarded." He twirled a pencil on his desk. "Fire alarm?"

"She'd have Alvar extinguish it. We have to lure her." Shayna should have made the capture when Kasdeya stood outside her motel room and watched the window. Shayna hadn't felt the time was right, but she wouldn't refrain from making the capture next time. If there was a next time.

"Demons don't have magic, right?"

Shayna nodded. "Alvar might have taught her a few minor spells, but she isn't capable of much."

"We need to make sure she's at the next battle, if we don't get to her before then." He set the pencil in a coffee mug, which held an assortment of pens and pencils. "Before would be preferable. History has shown soldiers don't do as well without a leader."

Unfortunately, they had no way of getting close to her. After Shayna had to rescue Deema from the demons' apartment, the shield around Kasdeya had been strengthened. They'd have to lure her out. "Has there been any trouble here?"

"Suspiciously quiet." He sighed. "I think you're the target. Yes, crime is still high and the vampires have caused some deaths, but the demon action increases when you're here."

"I'm no longer the queen." Her heart skipped a beat.

"But you are the strongest warrior." He folded his hands on the desktop. "With you out of the picture, Shayna, the other warriors will falter. You're their leader on the field, not Linette."

She jerked back in the chair. Pierce was right. Regardless of her pride, she'd have to accept the protection of her friends during a fight. Instead of stepping in front of them, she'd have to let them step in front of her. If one fell protecting her, she'd never survive the pain and guilt. "What can I do?" she forced the words through her tortured throat.

"Nothing." His eyes saddened. "We have to work harder at making sure nothing happens to you, because now that you're back and the other faeries escaped to safer grounds, the demon activity will increase."

She agreed. "Shall we go kick some demon butt? Let's make Alvar work harder at replacing the ones we destroy."

He laughed. "That's my girl." He stood and offered her his hand. "Let me do my best to protect you while fighting at your side."

"I will." No matter how much it went against her grain. "Where are the others?"

Before he could answer, Mary Ann, the receptionist buzzed the phone. Pierce answered, a stern look on his face. "Call SWAT," he said before hanging up. "We have a suicide bomber in the mall. We're going to need Agatha and her magic to save everyone."

They dashed from his office, calling to the others who waited in the break room. Agatha padded at Shayna's side, lifting her dark-eyed gaze to Shayna's.

"Bomber at the mall."

A hard glint shone in the witch's eyes. "Shall I transform to my regular form?"

"Not unless you have to. We need you kept as our secret weapon." Shayna patted her head. "Remember, no talking when we're around humans. Talking dogs aren't normal."

Agatha growled at a passing uniformed officer. The cop took a wide berth around them as he rushed outside.

"Behave. We need all the officers at their best." Shayna laughed and led her "dog" to a waiting van where Deema, Payson, and Marshal waited.

Deema's hard gaze stared out the window as Shayna explained about the theory of herself being the target. When Shayna finished, Deema faced her. "Then we make sure that doesn't happen."

Deema

As Shayna's protector, whether she was queen or not, Deema took the role seriously. When the van pulled up in front of the mall, she made sure to be the first one out. The others took her example, making sure to keep Shayna in the middle after her refusal to stay in the van.

"Deema, *shreank*." Shayna immediately became three inches tall.

Furious at not having the opportunity to talk her friend out of the strength-sapping transformation, she did the same. "What are you thinking?"

"That we need to get inside the building without being seen." She motioned to the blue-and-black butterfly ahead of them. "We need to catch up with Agatha."

"I don't like this," Pierce said, holding out his hand. "You could be captured."

Shayna landed in his palm. "I won't be." She blew him a kiss and flew off.

Deema landed on Payson's shoulder and placed a soft kiss on his neck. "We'll be back soon."

"Make sure you are or I'm coming in after you."

She laughed and followed the others to find a way into the strip mall, which consisted of an adult bookstore, a pharmacy, a chain department store, and a few clothing boutiques. Over a loud horn, Pierce ordered the evacuation of all stores. Customers and employees alike swarmed from all shops, except for the department store. Of course the bomber would choose the place with the most occupancy.

Deema caught up with the other two. "When did you cook up this idea?"

Shayna grinned. "Agatha and I came up with it in the van."

"So, that's what the whispering was about."

Shayna nodded. "Pierce and the others can't fight what they don't know. We're only here to scout the situation."

They squeezed in through an outside vent, stopping in what was obviously a stock room. Boxes upon boxes lined the walls along with racks full of clothing. Off to one side was a small restroom. Straight ahead were two swinging double doors with just enough space between them for the three to fly through.

"Do not be seen." Shayna said, "and make sure Agatha is kept safe. She has to revert to human size in order to cast any spells and now is not the time."

Deema nodded and placed herself between Shayna and Agatha. When a child darted from a rack of clothes and reached for the butterfly, Deema flapped her wings at his nose. The young boy cried and ran off in search of his mother. She hadn't harmed the child, only scared him.

The three perched on a shelf of coffeepots and blenders. Near the cash register, one man wearing a vest laden with explosives, held a gun on twenty customers and two staff members. A quick glance around showed several other customers and another staff member, hiding among the clothing. The crying child launched himself into the arms of a woman sitting with her back against the counter.

The bomber glanced in the direction the child had come, then turned his attention back to his hostages. "Shut that kid up."

Agatha fluttered away and hovered over the man's head, dropping blue dust on it before flying back to the shelf. Deema smiled. She knew tracking dust when she saw it. They would always know exactly where the bomber was.

Instead of landing on the shelf, Agatha reverted to her true form. "I have to stay," she said. "I'll do everything in my power to keep these people safe. Find the demons influencing that man and get rid of him." She moved quietly to the fringe of hostages and sat on the floor, pulling her cloak around her.

Shayna shot an angry look toward the witch before motioning for Deema to follow her. When they exited the store, she reverted to her full size. "Of all the obstinate people I've ever met, that one comes out on top."

"She knows what she's doing." Deema wished she felt as confident as her words sounded. Not even a witch could survive a bomb blast.

She stepped back from the building and squinted up at the roof. "I don't see them, but I know they're up there." She spotted a ladder leading straight up to the roof. "Shall we?"

"Don't let them see us until we're ready."

Deema jumped and gripped the first rung of the ladder and pulled herself up. The ladder shook as Shayna followed. Stopping just far enough that she could peer over the ledge, she whispered, "Six large demons are whispering words through the air conditioning. I don't think we can take them ourselves."

Shayna nodded. "We need the detectives and Earin. Let's head back."

After climbing down, they raced across the parking lot to the van. and Shayna explained the situation. "I'm summoning Earin. Agatha stayed inside to do what she could. Make sure the SWAT team doesn't shoot her." She handed an earpiece and small handheld device to Pierce, then whispered something in his ear.

His eyes widened as he placed the piece in his ear. "Are you sure?"

"Yes, but only when she says."

Deema feared she wouldn't like what Shayna and Agatha had planned and met Payson's worried gaze. "We can do this. Have the other officers work on keeping civilians away. It won't be an easy fight, but we'll win."

"Sure." He forced a smile. "With three faeries, one half-leprechaun, and two trained detectives, how can we lose?"

8
Deema

Earin arrived with two warriors and Nurse Zina. The nurse headed straight for the van. "I figured you could use the help. These are two of the most promising."

"We'd better not lose one of them." Deema switched to her armor. "You three will lead the charge with us following. Once up there, we form our fighting circle." She shot a glance at Shayna. "She must be protected at all costs. She's the target."

Earin nodded. "Understood. We'll follow your orders."

Shayna took a sip of the dragon's strengthening water she kept in her pocket, then handed it to Deema. "One sip only."

Knowing her weakness for the stuff, Deema nodded and sipped. Immediately the strength she'd lost from shrinking returned. "Douse your weapons with holy water," she told the others.

"Hold up, sir." Officer Charges handed Pierce a cellphone and glanced at Earin. "More special agents?" His gaze roamed over their bright clothing. "You don't believe in blending in, do you?"

Pierce clicked off the phone. "The bomber says to stop having the women run back and forth." He grinned. "They're a distraction. How about we keep him distracted? You two run across the lot. Hopefully that will draw the man to the window. The rest of us will circle around and meet you in the back. Ready?"

The group scattered. Deema and Shayna raced across the lot and behind the building where the men joined them a couple of minutes later.

"The only way up is that ladder," Deema said. "The first person up is going to be swarmed immediately. I'm first, so don't tarry." She reached for the rung, stopping when Earin grabbed her arm.

"Teleport as one."

She rolled her eyes. Of course. If she didn't make better decisions, they were all doomed.

"It's all right," Shayna said. "Just slow down. You can take charge just fine. We have faith in you."

Deema swallowed past a dry throat. "I liked it better when you took control."

Shayna gave a sad smile. "That cannot be right now." They each took the hand of the other and teleported, landing in the center of the roof.

Six demons hissed and charged.

The group formed their fighting circle. Despite

Shayna's protests of not being shoved to the middle, they closed in around her.

Zaps of blue zipped between their heads, striking the demons as fast as Shayna could cast the spells. War cries issued from Earin and the two warriors he'd brought as they raised their swords. Deema joined her cry with theirs and threw a dagger. It quivered as it struck its target. The demon vanished in a puff of dark smoke. Good. Alvar hadn't found a way around the demon's weakness to water.

Pierce followed suit, throwing knife after knife. Some hit, others didn't. Soon, they faced one angry demon who shouted curses at them. Before they could finish him off, three vampires appeared. Catching the group off guard, they surrounded Shayna.

"No." Deema left the remaining demon to the detectives. "Earin."

He whirled and leaped into the air, bringing his sword down through a vampire's head. He landed on his feet as Deema's were swept out from under her.

Shayna swung her weapon with two hands, removing the head from another before plunging the sword through its chest. Blood dripped from a scratch on her hand, another across her forehead. Still, she fought like the warrior she was.

Proud to follow such a one as she, Deema increased her attack. A vampire's sword caught her through the side, bringing her to her knees. One of the young warriors threw himself between her and the vampire, falling on the vampire's sword.

Deema staggered back, holding a hand to her side. Thank the Light they had an antidote for the poison coursing through her veins. With one hand, she tried to keep on the attack only to fall again.

With the demon disposed of, the three humans joined in the fight against the vampires. After a long and bloody battle with no one left unscathed, the warriors looked upon the body of the young man who had arrived with Earin.

"He gave his life for me," Deema said, kneeling beside him. She felt his neck for a pulse. "He is dead." Tears ran down her cheeks.

"Come, my love." Payson wrapped his arms around her waist and helped her to her feet. "We've got to get you medical attention."

"We all need it." Pierce had removed his shirt and pressed it to Shayna's head wound. "Earin, can you teleport us to the street?"

The faerie nodded. Soon they crowded around the van to the astounded looks of the other officers.

"What happened to all of you?" Officer Charges asked. "I know I'm not high up the ladder, but there is something definitely strange about these agents. Chief?"

"I'll let Agent Sky enlighten you."

Deema laughed, knowing the poor man wouldn't remember a thing about them appearing bloody and weary once she explained the situation to him. She lay on a cot in the back of the van and let the nurse pour some stinging solution on her side and something vile-tasting down her throat. When another sip of strengthening potion was offered, she took it gladly.

"If all the fights are going to be like that," Marshal said, "we're going to need more 'special agents.'" He glanced at Earin. "Sorry, about your warrior, man."

"Thank you. He died an honorable death. We will lose more before this is through."

Pierce

"What's happening, Agatha?" Pierce spoke softly into the hidden mic Shayna had attached to his collar.

"The sniper's settling down now that the demons are gone, but the crazed look in his eyes makes me nervous. It's as if he woke from a sleep and is now so frightened he's more of a danger than he was before. Wait for my call. He's holding a child in front of him. You'll have to have someone take the shot. Not a second before I say or we'll all blow."

This had to be the dumbest idea he'd ever heard. "We'll do our best." He kept his eyes on Shayna as the nurse tended her wounds and his attention returned to Agatha. Assured that Shayna would be fine, he stepped from the van, ignoring the nurse's protests that he had wounds that needed cleaning.

Once Agatha gave the go-ahead, not a second

could pass without the sniper pulling the trigger. The man stood behind a squad car, his rifle nestled on a tripod. "Do you have the bomber in sight?" Pierce asked.

"Yes, sir."

"Wait for my word, then no hesitation."

"There's an old woman standing too close."

"Disregard her. She's one of ours."

"Looks too old to be law enforcement, sir."

"She isn't, but she's helping. She knows the risks." Pierce squeezed his eyes shut. "You'd better not die, Agatha." He listened as she tried to convince the bomber to give her the trigger in his hand. The man refused.

"Take the shot on three, Pierce."

He ripped the device from his ear and held it to the sniper's. He grabbed a pair of binoculars and watched as Agatha cast a ray of yellow light at the bomber's trigger hand.

He glanced at his hand.

Agatha shoved the child away and put her hand over the bomber's.

The sniper squeezed the trigger.

The man fell.

Pierce held his breath.

Agatha held up the trigger in triumph.

Pierce put the earpiece back in his ear. "You're amazing for such an old woman."

"You ain't seen nothing yet, sweetie. A little freeze ray to hold the trigger in place was all it took. Now get these people out and the bomb squad in here. I'm ready to hand this over. The spell only lasts seconds."

His heart leaped into his throat as he motioned for the bomb squad to rush into the building. The hostages inside scrambled out, speeding toward the van.

"Don't you have a shield spell or something in case it goes wrong?"

Agatha laughed. "I'd be under that shield with the bomb. No thanks."

He watched as a man in a bomb suit carefully took the trigger from her hand while another dismantled the bomb on the dead man's vest. Pierce sagged against the van. First Shayna injured, then Deema stabbed, and now Agatha holding a bomb. These creatures from another world were amazing. He'd never been more thankful to have what little leprechaun blood he had.

Shayna joined him, her head bandaged and another around her hand. "It's over?"

"It's over." He smiled as Agatha marched from the building looking as fierce as any ancient witch could. "We owe that little lady our lives."

Shayna leaned her head on his shoulder. "Perhaps you should bind to her." She laughed.

"No, ma'am, I'm holding out for you." He put an arm around her shoulder.

"I need a drink," Agatha said. "Saving the world is hard work."

"We'll make sure you get all the whiskey you want as soon as all this is cleaned up," he promised. "I say we converge on Paddy's Pub. Ask him to close the place down except for us."

Agatha clapped him on the chest. "Now that's using your head. I'm going to go rest my bones."

She strolled to the back of the van and plopped onto a seat.

"How long do witches live?" he asked.

"This one won't live long enough for me." Shayna sighed. "I'll call Paddy and make the request." She stepped away from the commotion and borrowed a cell phone from Marshal. When she'd finished, she gave Pierce a thumbs-up, then placed a hand that glowed with a blue light on Agatha's shoulder.

Pierce's blood chilled. The old woman had been more taxed after the ordeal than she'd let on.

She put a hand over Shayna's and nodded. A moment later, she glanced Pierce's way and winked.

Relieved that Agatha would live to see another day, Pierce moved to the unpleasant task of making sure the freed hostages were taken care of and the building was deemed safe again.

"That was rough," Marshal said, falling into step beside him. "We almost didn't win this time. I'm afraid there might come a time when we won't. We could have lost one of the women or one of us. Or that witch."

"We all know the risks but can't step away from this." He'd once wished he'd never had his eyes open to the dark overtaking his city, but now realized he wouldn't change a thing. If Shayna hadn't come and convinced him to help, he'd never have met her. Anything was worth it as long as he fought by her side. "Do you need to move on?"

"Heck no. I'm a fighter. I love this city as much as the rest of you." He exhaled heavily. "I just wish there was a safer way."

"If you can think of a way for us to capture Kasdeya, I'll kiss you right on the mouth." He clapped Marshal on the shoulder. "Because that's the only thing that is going to get us past all this so we can destroy Abaddon."

"Right. Give me an impossible task." He glowered. "If you ever kiss me, I'll punch you."

"It would be worth it."

9
Shayna

The atmosphere at Paddy's filled with laughter, and for a short time, Shayna was able to sit back in the curve of Pierce's arm and pretend she was nothing more than an ordinary human woman. Not a warrior, not a faerie from another world, but a woman in love and spending time with her man. Their group, along with several leprechaun kin of Paddy's, crowded the pub and toasted with mugs of ale and glasses of champagne.

Weary from the worry over a store full of innocents, Shayna liked nothing more than to sit with those she cared for the most. Times of relaxation were few, and now that Linette had taken back her staff, a mountain of responsibility was removed from Shayna's shoulders. She lifted her lips for yet another of Pierce's kisses, tasting the ale on his lips. She'd stay here forever if only she could.

Agatha plopped down next to them. "A celebration this is."

"You wanted a drink." Shayna grinned, pulling away from Pierce. "Paddy will keep you supplied for the rest of your life. One of his cousins was in that store you saved, and he is more than grateful."

"I'm not a hero." She twirled an empty glass on the table. "I saved those people by saving myself."

"Not true." Pierce put his hand over hers. "Not many would tackle a suicide bomber the way you did. You took a great risk, one that we are all appreciative of."

Her face flushed. "I did it out of selfish means."

"How so?" Shayna peered into her face.

She shrugged. "I just want to be useful. All I do is sit in that hotel room all day unless you give me a job. Then, I'm as eager as a puppy being offered a treat. It's disgusting."

"You're right." Shayna put an arm around her. "We need a house. Somewhere with a yard so you can grow flowers and herbs and work on your spells. We'll pretend you're my grandmother."

"What about the other side knowing about me?"

"I no longer care. Let them know we have a witch more powerful than their pet faerie. Besides, my ancient friend, I'm quite aware of the fact that you can put a shield over the house and no one will be the wiser you're there."

"A toast to the witch!" Paddy's cousin cried.

"Here, here!" The room erupted in cheers.

Everyone fell silent when the vampires strolled in. Two men and one woman stood in the doorway, their eyes glowing red with hunger. "We heard there was a party," the woman said, showing her fangs. "Why weren't we invited?"

"It suddenly grew dark in here." Pierce tossed back the last of his drink and stood along with every other man in the room.

"Stay hidden, Agatha. Do not reveal what you are." Shayna withdrew her sword and joined Deema, standing among the three intruders and those celebrating. "Your invitation must have gotten lost." Couldn't they have one day without being harassed?

"We aren't here to fight this time," she said. "Although the scent of fae blood makes me ravenous. Alvar wants to speak with you. Alone."

"Alone won't happen." Deema moved in front of Shayna.

She shrugged. "Fine, but my friends here will stay and make sure no one other than you two leave this building."

Shayna smiled. "These men can take your two friends easily."

"I said we weren't here to fight. Are you coming or not?"

Shayna glanced at Deema, then to Agatha who nodded. "Yes, we're coming." Agatha had her back. Alvar wouldn't be able to harm her as long as Agatha was able to cast spells. As Shayna stepped outside, she felt the warmth of Agatha's shield drop over her.

Alvar and Linc sat on a bench outside the pub, standing when the three women joined them. "Nice work on stopping the bomber," Alvar said. "Who was the old woman?"

"Someone caught in a difficult situation. A very brave person." Shayna crossed her arms. "What do you want?"

"You, not to be too forward. Stop this madness and come with me. No one else will be harmed."

"Go with you and what...wait for you to kill me or turn me?"

He tilted his head to the side and gave a sly smile. "My dear, no. I will one day rule this world. With your power and mine...we'll be invincible. All I need to do is show you what can be yours if you join our side."

Shayna shook her head. "That will never happen. The next time we speak will be on the battlefield." She turned back toward the pub.

"Think about it, Shayna. With your fierceness and beauty, my magic combined with yours, we'd be unstoppable."

She stopped and glanced back. "Does Kasdeya know of your plans to oust her?" She flashed a grin and entered the building.

Did he seriously believe she'd change sides? The faerie's ego seemed to grow with each passing day. Since she was no longer queen, had he decided to capture her and force her to rule at his side? Because the target on her back had not gone away. There were ways a faerie with his skill at magic could brainwash even someone as strong as Shayna.

"He won't get to you." Deema slid her sword back in its sheath.

"He'll try to control my mind if he can't physically capture me." She laughed. "It wasn't wise of him to tell me of his intentions. Now, I can guard against anything he might try."

"What did he want?" Pierce asked when she sat back at the table.

"Me to rule at his side."

Agatha cracked up laughing. "It's a curse to be beautiful. I've never had the problem of men flocking around me. You've got two faeries and a human, lucky girl." She tapped Shayna on the nose. "I'm being facetious. I wouldn't trade places with you for anything."

Shayna frowned. "All faeries are beautiful."

"You're also wise, discerning, and a fierce warrior," Deema said. "Add that to your beauty and you're very desirable."

"You're the one that steals my heart." Payson placed a kiss on the top of Deema's head. "Even if I'm the only one who wants you." He laughed and dodged her playful punch.

Deema

All fun and joking aside, Deema knew the danger Alvar posed to Shayna was very, very real. Strong magic was dangerous. Agatha would be their only hope in keeping Shayna safe from mental attacks. She turned to look at the witch. They'd also have to keep her safe. If she fell, well, Deema wasn't sure she could protect Shayna on her own.

"What?" Agatha glared. "Do I have a wart on my nose?"

"She's worried about you," Shayna said.

"Stop reading my mind." Deema gestured for an ale. "You won't like it when I'm able to return the gesture." Some skills lost when following the dark took a long time to return. Reading minds in the human world was one of them.

"It's not something I can control."

"It is annoying," Pierce agreed, giving Shayna a one-armed hug, "but I've learned to keep my most private thoughts to myself until I'm alone."

"Is this gang-up-on-Shayna day?" Shayna glanced around the table. "You wouldn't do this if I were still queen."

"For which we are grateful." Deema raised the glass handed to her. "Hail to our non-queen, Shayna."

The room erupted again in cheers and laughter. Deema intended to enjoy the day, knowing danger lurked outside, waiting for them to let down their guard. The vampires and Alvar had known better than to attack a room full of fae who followed the Light, but they wouldn't hold back when Deema's smaller group separated from the rest.

She glanced at the front doors where night fell on an already gloomy day. The street lamps fought bravely to dispel the dark and failed. This kind of darkness needed a different light altogether.

A few humans peered into the pub, turning away when they spotted the sign that said reserved party only. What a wonderful place it would be if fae and human could live openly with each other.

"That will never happen," Shayna said. "The humans frighten too easily and would be as wary of us as we are of them when they enter our world."

"I know. It's best we protect them in secret." Under the table, she slipped her hand in Payson's and squeezed. "Except for you."

"My dark faerie princess." He kissed her.

"I'm no princess."

"You are to me."

Happiness bubbled in her like the seltzer water Shayna drank. One glass of champagne and their leader had switched to water. Not Deema. The human's liquor didn't affect her, but she enjoyed the taste.

Seamus appeared in the center of the table, a shower of gold flakes drifting in a puddle at his feet. "Did I miss the party?"

"Just getting started." Agatha wiped her spilled drink with the corner of her robe. "Get off the table, little man."

"Old nag." He hopped to the floor.

"Hold on, Seamus." Shayna grabbed the hem of his coat before he could scurry away. "Where have you been?"

"A drink first." He clapped his hands. "A whiskey, Paddy, my boy!" The dwarf shoved a stool to the table and climbed up. "While you all have been partying, I've been visiting me kin. It isn't good."

Deema leaned forward. "Explain, please."

He held up his hand for his drink, sipped, then

spoke. "America is not the only place where the darkness is spreading. It's creeping over the emerald lands of Ireland at an alarming rate. We don't have the resources to fight it. Not enough leprechauns. We're dropping like gold coins poured from a barrel. The good news…we're recruiting like mad."

Deema's heart froze. "An entire island of people will be converted. We'll never beat that number of undead."

Seamus tossed back the last of his drink. "I've no idea what to do except plead with the other races to join forces with us. I visited Queen Linette and was denied any warriors due to the fact they're in training and will be needed in the final battle. I've a few sprites and gnomes on me side, but tisn't enough. And…" he gave a devilish grin, "we've one bonny giant who is kept busy smashing vampires."

"What about your priests?" Pierce folded his arms on the table. "Ireland's got quite a few. Have all the clergy take blessing water and use your firetrucks to cover everything in sight. If there's nowhere for the vampires to hide, they'll leave."

"Silver on every doorpost wouldn't hurt either," Shayna added, before glancing at Deema. "Go with Seamus and return in the morning to let us know the severity of the situation in Ireland. We'll think of some way to help the Irish."

10
Deema

Before Deema could protest, Seamus grabbed her hand and teleported them to Dublin. She yanked free the moment her booted feet hit the cobblestones. "I should have some say in where I go."

"Well ye don't, so make the most of it." He set off as fast as his short legs would move. "Don't dawdle. We don't want them to know you're here." He ducked between two stone buildings leaving her with the option to stand on the sidewalk or follow. She chose the latter.

Seamus led her through a faded green door and up a flight of stairs to a second floor. At the top, he rapped out a complicated pattern of knocks and tossed Deema a wink. Within seconds the door swung open.

They stepped into a room full of dark and red-haired men and women. Whiskey flowed freely, a few danced a jig in the corner, and all stopped to stare when Seamus cleared his throat.

"I've brought the solution to our problem," he said, hopping onto a chair. "Meet Deema."

"Who is she?" One woman planted her fists on her hips. "Doesn't look very tough."

"She's the third strongest faerie in this world. At the moment, anyway." Seamus clapped Deema on the shoulder.

"Who is stronger than me other than Shayna?" Deema scowled.

"Why Earin, of course. No offense, love."

"He isn't," she muttered. Someday she'd prove she was stronger.

"So, what's she going to do for us?" Someone yelled.

"I'm here to advise you what to do, then I'll return to America where I'm needed the most." Deema told them of Pierce's idea of holy water and silver on the doors. "It wouldn't hurt for every one of you to carry silver weapons, either."

"We prefer gold!"

"Gold is useless against vampires." Deema looked as stern as she could. "If this island falls, then so will the rest of Europe, then Asia, and so on. The dark cannot win, my gold-loving friends. Recruit all you can. Even humans, if you must." She raised her hands against their protests. "Only if you must, and be selective of whom you choose."

"Want to see the sprites?" Seamus wiggled his eyebrows. "They're a rowdy bunch, so we've asked them to stay in the other room."

Rowdier than the leprechauns? Hard to imagine.

"Ryan, get started on finding silver and as many clergymen as you can gather. Make up whatever excuse you think they'll believe." He clapped his hands. "Chop chop. We've all got work to do." He opened a door in the back wall and swept his arm in a bow. "I'd introduce you, but they have no names."

Deema's eyes widened. He'd said a few sprites. The room teemed with them, three-foot high, blue creatures with wings. They all looked the same. Deema couldn't tell which were male and which were female. The air hummed with their song. They floated in mid-air at the sight of Deema.

One creature wearing a gold crown approached. "I remember you from the battle. It's good to see you again."

"The pleasure is all mine. There sure are a lot of you."

The sprite shook its head. "This is only a portion. The others are out recruiting or staying undercover until needed. We promised at the beginning to come when called, and we keep our promises."

"We appreciate that."

"They're quite the sight when converging on a vampire," Seamus said with a chuckle. "Bolts of lightning from their tiny fingers. Doesn't kill the vamps, but it does keep them busy until someone with stronger magic arrives. Wait until you see our gold vampire. Ryan touched her and turned her into a statue. Quite the sight."

"We're trying to figure out a spell that allows us to cast silver bolts of lightning," the leading sprite said. "We're getting close. The tide will turn for sure if we master it."

"I'll pray that you do." Deema smiled and turned to Seamus. "You don't need me. You have everything well under control. May I meet your giant?"

"The giant has gone to his people. Hopefully, he'll return to the moors with several willing to fight instead of staying neutral. I've brought ye because the leprechauns will have hope knowing the faerie is willing to help us as we've helped you in the past." He shrugged. "Queen Linette's refusal to lend us some of her warriors dashed a few hopes. I beg your forgiveness in my minor falsehood."

"Surely you understand her reasoning."

"Aye, but hope is still needed here in abundance. Sometimes, there isn't enough whiskey to fill everyone's hope tank." He laughed and rubbed his hands together. "Speaking of whiskey, let me buy you a drink and introduce you to a gnome. Caution, Ennis is quite the ugly fellow."

"I've never met one. What can he do?"

"Move underground like a mole undetected and manipulate the elements. I've seen Ennis toss a boulder the size of an elephant, and that's no lie." He led her back down the stairs and through another hallway before opening a plain wooden door to a room without windows. "They can't be exposed to sunlight. It turns them to stone."

"Ennis, I've someone for you to meet." Seamus flicked a light switch.

A one-foot creature wearing a brown hooded cloak scampered across the floor, his face as weathered and brown as a walnut. "Ah, a faerie, and a lovely one at that." His voice sounded as if he spoke through a mouthful of pebbles.

Deema bent closer to his level. "It's nice to meet you, and we're pleased you're joining the side of the Light."

He laughed. "Funny since sunlight is our enemy." He slapped his knee. "Just joking. Not about the sunlight, but we've never been ones to like evil."

"Are there many of you?"

"Thousands, my lovely." He hopped on a child-size chair. "We scamper here and there, alerting the good to the whereabouts of the evil. Never you fear, we'll be there when the time comes, but can only fight under the cover of darkness." His features saddened. "I've heard your city is fairly dark now, which will work to our advantage. I'll send some to your aid soon."

"It is dark. We'll welcome you with open arms."

Shayna

"We have gnomes?" Shayna said the next morning with a grin. "I've only heard stories of their incredible strength."

"Seamus said he saw Ennis toss a boulder the

size of an elephant." Deema sat in the nearest chair and glared at Agatha.

Talking was difficult over the wailing of sirens and squealing of tires from a television show the witch watched. Shayna did her best to ignore the noise. "They'll be a worthy asset. The sprites?"

"Perfecting their craft. Ireland will be all right." Deema grabbed the remote and lowered the volume. "Do you need a human hearing aid, old woman?"

Agatha snatched the control back. "Hush or I'll turn you into a toad."

Shayna understood the others' short tempers. She felt a bit stir crazy herself with no sign of demons or vampires since the previous day. "Let's go house hunting."

"Good." Agatha turned off the television. "I need a yard." She turned into a rottweiler. "Not because of my disguise, but I'm itching to get my hands in the dirt again. A concrete jungle loses its appeal quickly to one who loves trees."

Outside, they hailed a taxi. Remembering the name of the city Pierce had once thought Shayna came from, she ordered the cab driver to take them to Glen in the upper part of the state. The further they got from New York City, the more pleased she was with her decision.

Trees and grass everywhere. The darkness that covered the larger city they'd left behind had not reached the small community yet. It would be the perfect place to regroup and hide Agatha.

They found a two-story, white house with a wraparound porch and two chimneys on five acres of land. It was perfect. Shayna told the local real estate agent she wanted the house. By the end of the day, she had her wish.

"Must be nice to pay cash," the realtor said. "Not many can in today's age."

Shayna smiled and accepted the offered key. "Thank you." She turned and surveyed her humanly home once the realtor drove away. "Agatha, it's time for a charm."

Agatha ducked behind an oak tree and transformed back into herself. She raised her hands and slowly created a shield that matched the sky above them. Anyone flying over would see only clouds, sky and trees. The horizontal shield around the area showed only land without a house. No one would be allowed entry unless invited, and they wouldn't be able to see any part of the house. The dear old witch would be as safe as they could make her.

"We'll leave you now," she said, "and return this evening."

"I'll cook up a delicious meal in that wonderful kitchen." Agatha grinned. "Look, already forest creatures are coming to welcome me." A squirrel and rabbit scampered around her feet.

"That would be wonderful. Please make sure there is coffee." Shayna smiled and grabbed Deema's hand, transporting them to the back of the precinct.

A drunk blinked up at them. "That was cool. Not there, then there." He stared at the bottle in his hand. "Totally amazing."

With an amused glance, she decided to leave his memory intact, if he even remembered when he sobered up. Shayna opened the door and entered. Inside, she headed toward Pierce's office while Deema went to where Payson's desk sat in the bull pen.

"Hello, chief." Shayna sat in a chair and propped her crossed ankles on the desk.

"Hello, gorgeous. You look pretty happy."

"I bought a house in Glen and left Agatha there to cook and make coffee."

"That's great news. What else?" He sat back in his chair. "I can tell there is more."

"Lots more. Lots of gnomes, and sprites, and leprechauns…"

His eyes sparkled. "Our side is growing."

"By numbers I had only dreamed of."

He exhaled sharply. "So is the dark. I've had two vampire murders today and three disappearances. I'm assuming the missing have been converted."

"Deema and I will rid the city of a few every day if we can find them. They're staying suspiciously out of sight. You spoke only of the undead, not the demons?"

"No sign of them, large or small. It worries me."

Shayna steepled her fingers under her chin. "Me, too." What was Kasdeya up to? Had Alvar already taken control of Abaddon's forces and lay in wait until he had more creatures than could be counted? It might be time to pay a stealthy visit to Alvar's lair in the Circle of Mushrooms.

"Don't do it."

She raised her eyebrows.

"Whatever is going through your head, don't do

it."

Shayna laughed. She'd do whatever she thought was needed, and he knew it. Silly man. "No promises."

"Yeah." He shook his head. "You're hopeless as far as staying out of trouble."

She reached across the desk and put her hand over his. "No more so than you. That's why we make a good team."

"Yeah, because we aren't smart enough to stay where it's safe."

11
Deema

"Something smells good." Deema grinned upon entering the kitchen.

Agatha stirred something on the stove. Spread across every available surface were books, bottles, and dried herbs. "Don't eat it. It's not ready and will most likely kill you."

Marshal stopped his forward progression toward the stove. "What are we eating then?"

"You'll have to order a pizza. I've been busy trying to save your rear ends."

"Doing what?" Deema glanced into the pot of boiling dark brown liquid.

"Making potions." She turned a page in a nearby tattered book. "If I do this right, you'll get your ability to shoot lasers back sooner rather than later, and the humans will be faster and stronger."

"I'm not drinking that." Marshal sat at the table.

"You wanted to eat it a few minutes ago." Agatha turned and waved a wooden spoon at him. "Order that pizza, then go stand on the sidewalk and wait for it. You'll drink this potion when I tell you to."

Grumbling, Marshal shuffled from the room.

"You can actually improve the men's physical capabilities?" Deema glanced at Payson. "Is it safe?"

"No idea. Now leave me alone." Agatha turned back to the stove.

Shrugging, Deema joined Shayna and Pierce who whispered over a hand-drawn map. "What are you two cooking up?"

"I'd planned on going to the Circle of Mushrooms alone, but if that potion works, I'll take Pierce." Shayna pointed to a section of the map. "We need to find out why the demons have made themselves scarce."

"You plan on leaving me here?" Deema crossed her arms. Why would Shayna leave behind a warrior far more capable at protecting her than a human?

"Someone needs to stay behind in case I don't make it back." Shayna lifted a worried gaze. "That is a great possibility with such a risk. Other than myself, you're the only one that can watch the others."

"Then let me take the risk."

She shook her head. "Alvar won't kill me, but he won't think twice about ending your life."

Deema still didn't understand the reasoning. "But you'll take Pierce."

"He won't let me go alone, and I will not risk my best warrior on an errand that may result in nothing." Shayna's gaze hardened. "I've made my decision, Deema."

"Ugh." Deema stormed outside and stared at the sky. Storm clouds gathered, pregnant with rain and dark smoke. A slight breeze ruffled Deema's hair. Thankfully, they were signs made by nature and not demons.

Outside of the shield, pacing the sidewalk, Marshal waited for the pizza delivery. He'd have to come up with a good explanation for waiting in a spot that appeared to have no house.

The detective didn't speak much in the group, keeping to himself, but he never backed down from a fight, and Deema respected that. Shayna said he harbored jealousy and fear, but Deema couldn't see it. He'd stopped requesting a faerie protector of his own weeks ago, although loneliness rolled off him in waves. Deema pierced the barrier and joined him.

"Nice evening," she said.

He stopped his pacing. "I suppose. Strange, though, don't you think that we've not had to fight in a few days? Nor have we heard any word of Kasdeya. Can demons be redeemed? Maybe she's had a change of heart."

Deema hadn't expected that question. "Maybe if they're returned back to their human state. I'm not sure. Why do you ask?"

"I've been thinking while I waited out here about what we know, or at least strongly suspect, about Alvar wanting to take over the dark side. What if Kasdeya turned to us?"

"I'm not following." Why would someone with her power want to join the Light and lose it all?

"What if someone told her of Alvar's plans? She'd see the dark side's deceit. Maybe that would be enough to convince her that our side is the right one."

"You're expecting a lot, Marshal. Those in the dark don't often come back."

"You did."

"True, but I remained my true form. Kasdeya didn't. She lost her humanity when she accepted the role of demon."

"But she's still human, right? Possessed or something similar?" He resumed his pacing. "I've heard stories of people possessed by demons. What if that is the case here? That means she can be saved."

Deema sighed. "Why is this so important to you? Kasdeya made her choice a long time ago."

He stopped at the curb as a pizza delivery car pulled up. "There's something about her I can't explain." He paid the driver and headed for the house. "A look on her face when I caught her watching Shayna's apartment. Something vulnerable."

"Don't put your hope where it does no good," she said, following him.

"Shayna said there is always hope." Without a backward glance, he entered the house, leaving Deema alone on the porch.

Kasdeya leave her position of power for one of a lowly human? Deema couldn't see it. When she'd been captured and held in a glass jar on the demon's sideboard, she'd seen firsthand the element of evil in the woman's heart. Black as night and as thick as the moss in a swamp, Kasdeya grasped the darkness with both hands and held tight.

She opened the front door and made her way back to the kitchen. From the laughter and friendly jests of them all fighting over which slice of pizza they wanted, it didn't appear as if Marshal had told the others his thoughts. He glanced up at Deema without speaking, then turned away.

Point taken. She'd not say anything either. All she could do was hope the man didn't do anything stupid.

Pierce

"Done." Agatha ladled some of the now vile-smelling liquid into a coffee mug. "Who wants to be a guinea pig?"

"Literally or figuratively?" Pierce tossed his napkin onto his paper plate. "I guess I will since I'm the one going with Shayna tomorrow."

"Deema, you too." Agatha made another cup. "Then you can go outside and practice shooting."

Pierce glanced at Deema. "I'll go first. Just in case it kills me." He tossed Agatha a wink and downed the contents of the mug as fast as he could.

"That's nasty." He shuddered. "Not that I've ever drank skunk spray, but I bet this is what it tastes like."

"Do you feel any different?" Shayna asked.

"No." Except his stomach threatened to return what he drank. "Just nauseous."

Deema drank hers. Her body convulsed. Her fingertips turned purple almost immediately. When her body stilled, she smiled. "Look at this." She pointed her finger at the table and shot the pizza box across the surface and onto the floor.

"How will I know if it worked?" Pierce glanced at his hands. While he could make his palm glow green and telepathically throw knives, he couldn't shoot anything from his fingertips.

"Go run around the yard." Agatha removed the frilly yellow apron she wore and hung it on a peg. "You'll know."

They all converged outside, everyone but Pierce and Deema sitting in rockers on the back porch. Run around the yard? Okay, fine. Pierce leaped off the porch and took off.

"Yeehaw!" He sprinted at twice his normal speed, leaping with ease over anything that got in his way.

"Dodge this." Deema shot a purple laser at him.

He stopped on a dime. The laser missed him by inches "Now, that's cool." He laughed as Payson and Marshal tried to run through the back door at the same time in their rush to take the potion.

"You, too, Shayna." Agatha handed her a cup. "It'll prevent your mind from being controlled." The witch grinned. "I've outdone myself this time.

While all of you will be stronger, it also enhances your best attributes and makes you resistant to influence of any kind." She reached over her shoulder and patted herself on her back. "Oh, and you might want to call a plumber. My first two batches ate through the kitchen pipes when I dumped them out. We can't do the dishes or wash our hands."

Pierce threw back his head in laughter. He'd never felt better in his life, nor loved anyone more than he loved this group of warriors. He picked up a rock the size of his fist and threw it over the house. Amazing. He sat on the porch next to Shayna who stared at the cup without drinking.

"Do it fast. That's the best way." He took her free hand. "This had better prepare us for whatever the future might throw our way."

"I know, but…" she locked gazes with him. "It ruined the pipes, and she wants us to drink this vile stuff."

"Not this batch," Agatha said. "The ones I messed up on were too strong." Her grin faded, and she glanced overhead. "I hope you didn't put a hole in the shield when you threw that rock, Pierce, because we've visitors coming fast." Gathering her robes around her bony knees, she darted from the porch and around the corner of the house.

Shayna gulped back her drink and took off after the old woman. Pierce followed, just in time to see Agatha patch a hole in the shield.

"That was close." She took a deep shuddering breath. "I sensed at least ten of the undead. They're prowling, looking for us.

"Are you sure they don't know we're here?" Pierce glanced up.

"A body can never be sure of anything, but I'm pretty certain. If they did know, they'd have broken through the hole and attacked. I sensed them but didn't see them. They weren't close enough. We're safe this time."

By the time they returned to the back yard, Payson and Marshal were racing each other from one side of the yard to the other while Deema zapped rays of purple at them. "Will she hurt them if she hits?" Pierce frowned.

"She's using stun," Shayna said, smiling. "You're all like a bunch of children at a party."

He pulled her close to his side. "You're used to all this. We aren't. Come on. Let's go make plans to leave in the morning." Nervousness still threatened to make his knees weak, but he felt a lot more ready to face whatever they'd find tomorrow then he'd felt an hour ago.

Payson and Marshal leaped over the porch railing and back into the house where they promptly set up a competition of arm wrestling.

Deema laughed. "I've not seen Marshal this excited since I met him."

Without letting up on Payson, he said, "I've not received anything cool since this whole thing started until now. Payson has you, Pierce has Shayna, now I've got something even if it won't keep my bed warm at night."

Pierce clapped his partner on the shoulder. "You'll find love, dude. Just wait until this battle is won. It's a bear having to worry about the love of your life dying, anyway." He cut Shayna a sideways glance. She'd put him in his place if she heard their conversation. Thank goodness for Agatha's shield of protection. No mind reading was allowed.

"I know. I see how it affects you and this weak guy here."

Neither man's arm budged, nor did their grip loosen. Pierce laughed. "You'll be here all night. See you in the morning." He joined Shayna at the table and leaned over her shoulder. "I gather from the distance this is from The Glen, that we have to ride Gorna again."

"Yes. If they haven't left. I've not been able to connect with her since the evacuation. We'll stop at The Glen first, then try and find her." She rolled up the map. "You'd best get some sleep, love. Tomorrow could be a very long day."

Or two.

12
Shayna

Shayna woke before dawn and stood next to Deema's bed. "If you are discovered, protect Agatha at all costs. She's the key to our victory."

Deema sat up, glancing at the sleeping Payson. "I beg to differ. I believe you're the key, but I will keep her safe or die trying." She stood and clasped Shayna's hands. "Please return to us."

"I plan on it." Shayna smiled, then pulled her friend close for a hug. "May the Light be with you."

"And you."

She released Deema's hands and joined Pierce in the yard. "We need to get to the portal before daylight. We cannot be seen and alert the other side."

"Agreed." He took her hand. "Let's do this."

She teleported them to Central Park, then led

him through the portal and into The Glen. With twice as many faerie living in the valley, the trek to the throne room took twice as long as usual. Every walkway presented a challenge as she had to squeeze through pedestrians and running children. Still, the smile didn't leave her face. One faerie race again together in one place instead of divided with miles between them.

Finally, she and Pierce stood in front of the two queens, who for a time at least, agreed to rule side by side. Shayna bowed. "We are going on a scouting mission to the Circle of Mushrooms. I'm concerned that I haven't been able to connect with Gorna. Her assistance would make the journey easier."

Linette smiled. "That's because the dragons have a shield over them to prevent Alvar from knowing their present location. They've moved to the caves in our northern mountain range. Alas, you'll have to physically go there. The shield keeps out any telepathic connection until inside."

"Then, we shall take our leave." Shayna took a couple of steps backward.

"Stop by the kitchens first and have them pack you food and drink. This is not a journey that will happen in a day."

Shayna nodded again and left the throne room. One day's journey to the dragons, then a teleportation to the Circle of Mushrooms. Two days at the most before she and Pierce could return home.

"I hope the others can hold down the castle until we return," Pierce said.

"They can. As long as their location is kept secret."

"Payson and Marshal still have to work. I've put in for vacation time, so I'm good for a few days, but the precinct can't run on empty."

"I understand. We'll take Crystal as far as we can, but it will still take a minimum of two days." She cut him a look. "More if we're captured. You have to trust the ones left at home."

"I do." He took a deep breath. "Really."

She laughed. "You're as bad as I am at thinking no one can do it as well as we can." She shoved open the door to the kitchen. Two packs sat bulging on the marble counter. Linette had sent word ahead. She always seemed to know what Shayna needed before being asked. Slinging one of the packs over her shoulder, she headed to the stables and whistled for Crystal.

The winged horse glided to a stop in front of them. Shayna pressed her forehead to the horse's. "I've missed you, my beauty. Are you willing to carry two again?"

The horse snorted and pawed the ground.

"I'll take that as a yes." She swung onto the horse's back and held out an arm to help Pierce up. "Hold on tight."

"I know the drill." He wrapped his arms around her waist as Crystal rose into the sky.

The sun sat directly overhead by the time they'd gone as far as they could. The shield stopped them from going any further except on foot. After sending Crystal back to The Glen, Shayna put her hands on the invisible barrier. "*Entrae.*" A space just large enough to walk through appeared in front of them.

Once inside, the shield closed back together. Shayna stared up at a mountain, so tall its tip disappeared in the clouds.

"Where's the entrance?" Pierce followed her gaze.

"Up there. We've some climbing to do."

"Great."

Grappling for foot and handholds took every ounce of physical strength Shayna possessed. By the time they located the entrance to the caves inside the massive mountain range, her limbs trembled. In the human world, her strength rarely waned, unless injured. Here, she was no different than a human was in their world. Exhaustion coated her like a heavy wet blanket.

"A breather." Pierce collapsed on a patch of moss. "Beautiful place but rugged. At least we won't have to climb down."

Shayna agreed wholeheartedly. She lay back with him. Five minutes' rest wouldn't hurt.

She woke to hot breath on her face.

Pierce yelped and bolted upright.

Gorna stared down at them, a twinkle in her gold-colored eye. "It's good you found me."

"You scared a hundred years off me." Shayna placed her hand flat on the dragon's neck. "I'm in need of your assistance again. We need a ride to the Circle of Mushrooms."

"It's a dark place now and overrun with evil."

"They've taken the city?"

Gorna nodded. "Queen Brigette will never be

able to restore it to its former beauty. Are you sure you wish to go?"

"Can you get us there unseen?"

"Most definitely." She turned toward Pierce.

"I wish I understood dragon talk," he said. "I feel as if she wants to barbeque me."

Shayna laughed. "She prefers her meat raw." She climbed onto the dragon's back and waited until Pierce joined her.

"I have been so far out of my comfort zone since meeting you in that alley."

"You've made my world better." She nudged Gorna with her knees and off they flew. Tomorrow would be a dark day full of danger. She was grateful to have Pierce by her side.

Deema

"With the chief gone, we have to go into the city." Payson put on his shoulder holster, then donned a jacket. "You have to stay here and guard Agatha."

"She can turn into a dog and we all go." Deema scowled. "We're safer together. The enemy wants to divide us. I won't allow it to happen."

Payson pinched the bridge of his nose. "This may be our first argument."

She stepped behind him and wrapped her arms around his waist. "Shayna left me in charge. Trust me."

He turned. "I do. You're right. We'll stay together. How will we get to the precinct without being seen?"

"The long way. By cab." She'd already thought it through. They'd call a cab, have Agatha watch for its arrival, then rush inside the car once it arrived. They'd be in the open seconds at the most. It would work. It had to.

She told Agatha of the plan. The witch pondered for a moment, then nodded. "It'll work. No one will know we are out there unless they see us. I can't set another charm while under this shield. I can do it right away outside, but I'd have to be in my true form."

"We'll do without the charm and make haste." Deema made eye contact with the others. "Call the cab. Agatha, keep watch."

While Agatha paced on the sidewalk, nosing around like a dog when let loose, Deema stood just inside the shield with one hand on her sword in case of trouble. Payson and Marshal stood on each side of her like stoic bookends. She scanned the sky for any sign of darkness, breathing a sigh of relief when the cab pulled up to the curb. The four of them were inside the vehicle within two seconds.

Deema exhaled the breath she'd held and rested her head against the seat back. They'd done it. Now to get inside the precinct without their enemies knowing Shayna was not with them.

As they neared their destination, she leaned

forward. "Don't stop." On the steps of the precinct waited two vampires. Two more paced the sidewalk. "Go around to the back and pull as close to the building as you can get."

The driver glanced in his rearview mirror. "You on the run?"

"Something like that. Except we're running into the police station. Do you have a blanket?"

"Under the seat, but it'll cost you twenty."

"Really? What happened to helping out your fellow man?" Marshal pulled a twenty-dollar bill from his pocket and handed it to the driver. "Here's another twenty to keep your mouth shut. No one needs to know we have a celebrity here." He winked at Deema.

The driver's eyes widened. "I can keep a secret." He kept his gaze on Deema. "I think I recognize you from a movie or something."

"Or something." Deema pulled the blanket from under the driver's seat. "We'll put this over us. Unless they count legs, they won't know how many of us there are. Make it fast."

They flung open the door and darted inside the building to the questioning look of two male vampires. Since they didn't attack, they obviously were none the wiser.

"Smart thinking." Payson grabbed Deema for a kiss. "You too, Marshal. Good way to explain our secrecy."

"I've got a few ideas swimming around in my head on occasion." He led the way to the bullpen, stopping by the receptionist desk on the way.

She glanced up. "Everything has been sent to

your email. Nothing major. Isn't that strange for this city? One day we have more crime than we can handle, barely any the next."

"It is strange, but let's count our blessings." He flashed her a smile, then turned to the others. "Hopefully, we can stay safe inside."

Agatha huffed and lay down, resting her chin on her paws. The look in her large brown eyes clearly said she wasn't happy about being cooped up inside.

"I wonder how Pierce and Shayna are doing." Payson sat at his desk and turned on his laptop. "For a while we had so much going on that now it's boring just to sit. I really wanted to try out my new talents."

"Shh." Deema glanced at Officer Charges. "No talking unless you can explain what you're talking about. Might be difficult."

After an hour of nothing, Deema got up to pace the room. Uniformed officers came and went, but with no deaths or violent crimes, the detectives weren't needed. What was going on? She sidled to stare out the front glass doors.

A total of ten vampires now wandered the area, some sitting on benches, others pretending to be in conversation and hungrily eyeing any pedestrian that walked by. Things were definitely not normal, and Deema's heart picked up a beat. Something big was coming. Something that would happen when Shayna and Pierce returned. Right now, the undead seemed to be on a scouting mission.

She glanced at the other three. Should they fight if needed or stay in the protection of the building?

Alvar couldn't draw them out or enter. With those outside, neither could her group. Their ruse at the back door wouldn't work a second time.

"What?" Payson glanced up, his brow furrowed.

"We're trapped."

13
Shayna

Gorna landed just out of sight of the Circle of Mushrooms, cutting through a sky as dark as ink. The dark had overtaken the once beautiful city ruled by Queen Brigette. Shayna's heart broke at the sight of so many large demons roaming the streets where once the faerie had lived and played.

"Alvar is definitely creating an army," Pierce said, sliding from Gorna's back. "We need to find a way to stop him."

She agreed but had no idea how to stop such a mass from taking over their worlds. The fight might not happen in the human world this time. If the fae lost, humanity's fate was doomed. She glanced at Pierce. His face showed the same worry that flooded through her.

"This is bad," Gorna said. "We can destroy the place where he creates these monsters, but we cannot attack this city. It's been protected from fire for centuries."

"Then go. Get the other dragons and destroy those caves. Pierce and I will handle things here." Shayna checked her weapons, doing her best to give Pierce the chance to back out, gain courage, whatever it was he needed to do in preparation for what was most likely a suicide mission.

Pierce's gaze followed Gorna's departure before turning to Shayna. "I hope you have a plan, because mine just flew away."

"She's getting the other dragons to destroy the caves. We're on our own until the dragons return."

He paled. "How long will that be?"

"Most of the day." She tried to smile and failed. "We need to find a way to sabotage Alvar and slow down his coming attack on The Glen."

"What if we can't? We're two people, Shayna, not an army."

"We're on a scouting expedition. The only plan I have is to gather information and get back out without being seen. I don't intend to engage."

"I like that plan." He tightened his belt. "Let's go. We've a bit of a walk, I'm guessing."

True. Gorna had dropped them several miles from the dark city. Hitching her pack more firmly on her shoulders, Shayna parted the foliage in front of her and started the trek. While the city sat on grassy plains, it held enough trees to provide an element of cover to their progression and enough hills to make the hike wearisome.

Halfway to the city, she stopped near a stream to rest and eat a bite of the food they carried. She toed off her boots and stuck her aching feet in the cool water.

"You're the same as me in your world," Pierce said, copying her. "You tire and ache after walking for miles. I'd thought you'd be as strong and invincible here as you are there."

She shook her head. "The faerie are still capable of quite a lot, but our physical strength has waned some in our world." She leaned back on her hands. The once crisp air smelled foul, the sun barely breaking through the gray clouds. The thick cloud cover was good at helping to keep them from being seen but hid much of the land's beauty.

"I wish you could see this place without the darkness." She faced Pierce. "It's almost as beautiful as The Glen."

He reached over and took her hand, squeezing lightly. "I'll get a chance. Even the smallest flicker of light can pierce the darkness. Hold on to that thought. The Light will return to this place."

She chuckled. "You've learned well."

"I had a good teacher." He pulled her close for a kiss, then grabbed his boots. "Break's over, gorgeous. Time to go."

Feet rested and hunger satisfied by nutritious bread, Shayna once again took the lead. She stopped a few hundred yards from the city's gate. Stretching before them was a wide-open meadow. The grass reached waist-high. The only way to avoid being seen would be to crawl. She glanced at the sky, then toward the hills where Gorna would be leading the attack.

"We wait here for the dragons to draw attention

to them. Then, we make haste across the meadow."

Pierce nodded. "What if the dragons don't show up?"

"They will." She sat cross-legged on the ground and kept her gaze on the sky. Gorna had let her know they were on their way.

"I haven't said anything, thinking the answer would come to me, but I've a question." Pierce leaned against the trunk of a moss-covered tree. "I know why we couldn't teleport to the dragons because of the shield, but why didn't we outside the city?"

"Magic leaves a trace. If we teleported, Alvar would know. If he knows we're here, he also knows we are not in New York, which leaves the others vulnerable to attack. There." She stood and pointed.

The dragons had arrived, flying in a V like large geese. They swooped overhead, blocking what little sunlight there was, then veered toward the hills. Seconds later, fire balls rained on the countryside. A mass of demons flew to intercept.

"Let's go. Stay low." Shayna darted across the meadow.

As they neared the city, she turned, hoping to find another way in besides the front gate. That, she knew, would be closely guarded. They didn't have long. Gorna warned that when the fight over the hills grew too dangerous, she'd swoop down to collect them. She needed to find Alvar and get a better idea of what the fae were up against.

There. A small gate in the side wall. She parted climbing ivy and slipped through with Pierce on her heels. Keeping to the shadows, she led the way to the palace and into the rooms underground where the chains for Abaddon had been forged. They'd be directly under the throne room.

Putting a finger to her lips, she moved to the center of the room, trying to find a way to hear what went on overhead. Hearing through the marble floor would be impossible. They headed upward, moving like turtles until a wooden door stopped them.

"We should attack now." Kasdeya's voice drifted through the spaces in the planks.

"We aren't ready," Alvar said. "We've more shifters arriving, and the vampires are still converting."

"Demons?"

"I think we have enough." He laughed. "Queen Linette's light magic will be tested against their strength."

"Sir!" Footsteps pounded across the floor. "Dragons are attacking the caves."

"Who's stopping them?" Alvar demanded.

"Your creatures flew to intercept, but they're dropping like flies."

Kasdeya's shrill laugh rang out. "Demons from hell that can't withstand fire? That's a hoot."

"Some abilities were obviously lost in the transformation." He cursed. "Now, I'm unable to replace the ones lost. Get your vampires working overtime. Have them attack the police station. Get someone to kill those dragons!"

"Holy water on the station, remember?"

"Find a way!"

Sounds of a scuffle, then Kasdeya's cold tone. "I'm in charge here. Remember that. You're nothing but a faerie, and I can burn you to a crisp with one touch of my finger if I should desire. Rather than storm and curse, I suggest you find a way to regroup and attack The Glen."

"We have to go," Shayna whispered, grabbing Pierce's arm. "Gorna is waiting. Hurry before she's detected."

They raced out the way they'd come, Alvar's cry of warning sounding behind them. "She's here. The precinct is unprotected."

With all the demons occupied fighting dragons, none were left to pursue Shayna and Pierce. They burst out into the open and leaped onto Gorna's back. She flapped her wings as Alvar burst through the gate.

A silver bolt shot from his fingertips, stinging Shayna's armor. She returned fire with one of her own and clutched one of Gorna's spikes in order not to fall. "Stay down, Pierce." She shot again over his head. Alvar dove back through the gate.

Deema

At least twenty vampires paced the sidewalk. Payson had ordered everyone in the building to remain inside. Officer Charges, already outside, was told to drive his car up and down the street telling pedestrians to stay inside until an all clear was given and not to get out of his car no matter what. Still Deema's heart dropped as two young men refused to follow orders and were quickly set upon by two of the vampires.

Payson stepped next to her. "What do we do?"

"We'll have to fight." They'd not survive. There weren't enough fighters of light. She sent a telepathic message to Earin. Hopefully, he could arrive in time.

"I'll have to let my presence be known," Agatha said, approaching them in her true form. "I'll have to fight with magic, and I cannot do that as a dog."

Shayna was going to kill Deema herself if anything happened to the witch. "I'm hoping it won't come to that. Isn't there any magic you can do from in here?"

"I can do a lot, but it will alert them to the presence of a witch."

"We have to do something," Marshal said. "People are dying. What would Shayna do?"

"Whatever needed doing." Deema glanced at Agatha, preparing to tell her to use her magic.

Shayna and Pierce appeared behind the witch. Deema had never been happier to see anyone than in her life.

"Well," Mary Ann said from behind the reception desk. "You folks must have forgotten I was here, because you're spilling all your secrets. I'm not the only one in the room with eyes to see and ears to hear." She motioned her head toward a couple of men brought in for drunkenness. They watched the proceedings with wide eyes. "Now, them…they probably won't remember a thing once they sober up." She stood and joined the faeries. "But me, I don't forget anything." She raised a finger and pointed at the clock. "No matter how much time has passed." The clock's hands spun so fast they were nothing more than a blur.

"You're a witch?" Agatha's mouth fell open.

Mary Ann smiled. "Yes. We've devised a spell to keep our identities secret even when using magic."

"We?" Agatha moved slowly toward the desk. "There are more?"

"A handful, but yes. We went into hiding over a century ago, choosing to stay out of this fight. But the faeries seem to have brought the fight to us."

"Which side will you choose?" Deema put her hand on the hilt of her sword.

"Relax. We practice white magic. Those who practiced dark are long gone. We made sure of that."

Agatha's eyes widened to learn she wasn't the last of her kind as she'd thought. "With a group of us, we'll be a formidable force."

"I'm not making any promises other than that I will speak with the others." Mary Ann returned to typing on her keyboard.

Deema glanced at Shayna. "Have you looked outside?"

She turned to the door, her features settling into a hard mask of anger. "We need to get rid of them."

"Agatha wants to fight. I was about to allow it when you arrived." Deema dared Shayna to argue. "I've also sent a cry for help to Earin. People are being converted right in front of us."

"Then we have no other choice. You did well." Shayna put a hand on her shoulder. "It's good to know I have such a warrior at my side."

Pride filled Deema with a warmth she hadn't felt in a long time. "It is my pleasure to serve you, my friend."

"Stop the gushy stuff." Agatha brushed her robes aside. "Time to fight. I'll rid the street of as many as I can, then leave the hand-to-hand combat to the rest of you."

"I told each of my girls to make their own decision," Mary Ann said, standing. "My choice is to fight. Step back and let us show you how it's done." She waved her left hand in a circle over Agatha's head and chanted something under her breath. "There. No one will know you're a witch unless you tell them."

Agatha grinned. "Except those vampires on the street. They need to be destroyed to keep our secret."

Deema stepped back from the door. "Ladies, do your magic." She moved to Payson's side, anxious to see what the two could do. A handful of witches. That was the best news she'd heard in days. The tide was turning.

Shayna stood between the two witches. "They must see me. They'll think all the magic comes from me. Not to take away your glory, but they know I'm strong in that field, and the longer your identity is hidden, the better."

"You're strong in all fields," Deema stated. "That's why you're the leader. Just give the rest of us the word when you want us to draw our swords." They were ready to turn those undead into nothing but ashes. Her fingers curled around the hilt of her sword, itching to fight.

14
Shayna

Shayna blasted the front doors open with a bolt of light, then held up her hands, palms facing out. A bright light emanated from them, driving the vampires further into the street.

Agatha and Mary Ann cast spell after spell shooting fire balls at the vampires. It didn't take the undead long to figure out Shayna wasn't the only one using magic. The ones not blasted by fire ducked behind cars and into the alcoves of store fronts. One of them shouted out that witches had joined the side of the Light.

"We discovered the new breed of demons can't handle fire," Shayna said. "Knowing the two of you are capable of doing what you just did will be an immense help. Deema, you and the others come forward now. Agatha, Mary Ann, step back. We don't want your magic hitting any of us." With her sword gripped in both hands, Shayna led the charge out of the building.

As if they'd been fighting together all their lives, the other four fanned out behind her, two on each side. Before they reached the street, Earin and two more warriors appeared.

"Heard there was a party happening." He flashed a grin.

"We're pleased to have you." Shayna directed everyone into a fighting circle in the center of the street.

The vampires circled like birds of prey, their eyes glowing red from their pale faces. They bared their fangs and pulled swords of their own from beneath black coats. Overhead, five of the new form of demons arrived.

"Do not break rank no matter what," Shayna said. "They'll try to separate us. Do not let that happen." She should have made sure everyone wore their necklaces. She could only hope they still kept them on at all times.

Kasdeya appeared on the opposite sidewalk barking orders like a drill sergeant. Those who followed the dark pulled back, not happy. They strained toward Shayna's group like dogs held on a tight leash. She said something else, and a few rushed forward in a tight group.

The vampires and demons spread out, making it two of them to every one of Shayna's group while the initial attack tried to distract. "No fear," she told the others. "We can take them."

The three humans uncorked their bottles of holy

water and tossed the contents into the faces of their attackers, effectively evening the odds. Bless Pierce for having barrels of the water stored in the precinct for easy refilling.

With claws out, the demons hissed and advanced, leaving the vampires standing a couple of feet back in waiting.

"They are more organized now," Deema said, slashing the head from the nearest demon. "Not as stupid."

"But still not smart enough." Shayna lunged forward, piercing one with the edge of her sword. Before she could pull free and send the creature back to the abyss it came from, one of the vampires attacked.

She thrust her left arm upward, protecting her neck. Fangs scraped the dragon scales protecting her. Shayna pulled her sword free of the demon's form. While its ashes still hung in the air, she stabbed her weapon into the chest of the creature attached to her arm.

"Kill them!" Kasdeya marched up and down the sidewalk, her fists clenched, her gaze boring into Shayna's. "Kill the blond first."

"That's the creature you think can be redeemed?" Deema shot Marshal a look.

There'd be questions later. As soon as they returned to her house, Shayna would want to know what Deema meant.

One of the faeries who had arrived with Earin fell. A vampire leaped on the fallen warrior. Shayna fought to the man's side as the vampire sank its fangs into his neck. No. She kicked out, knocking the undead from the injured fae, then disposed of it. "Earin. He must go to the infirmary immediately. Time is of the essence."

"You need my help."

"He must be saved. We will be fine."

With a nod, Earin grabbed the man's hand and disappeared.

Agatha growled and leaped, having reverted to dog form and joined the fight despite Shayna's orders to the contrary. She jumped on the fallen vampire and ripped off its head. Mary Ann sank a silver-tipped wooden stake into its chest.

At Shayna's curious look, she shrugged. "I can't change into anything, although that is a skill I'd like to have. I'll fight as a woman."

"Works for me." Shayna threw a dagger over the witch's shoulder, catching another vampire between the eyes.

Mary Ann might be fighting as a human woman wearing no armor, but her skill showed she'd had training in combat. More questions that needed answering.

Pierce had made his way to Shayna's side and threw knife after knife at the darting vampires. Thanks to Agatha's clever magic, the knives always returned to his outstretched hand to be thrown again with remarkable speed, due to the potion he'd drunk.

While the fight seemed to last much longer, only half an hour had passed before no more demons or vampires littered the street. Kasdeya narrowed her eyes from the opposite side. "You may win the minor skirmishes, Shayna, but we're learning your weaknesses. You will not win in the end. Congratulations on the witches, but even they will not help you win." She snarled and snapped her fingers as Deema raised her arm to throw her sword.

"She needs to die, that one." Deema's lips curled in a snarl.

"No." Shayna sheathed her sword. "Everyone, let's go to my place. Agatha, a spell of forgetfulness on those watching from the stores, please." Once the witch complied, Mary Ann requested Shayna's home address, saying she'd arrived later with or without the others. Then, holding hands, the rest teleported to Shayna's. The lone warrior of Earin's went home to check on his comrade.

"Man, that was a rough one." Inside the shield, Marshal leaned against the porch. "I hope they don't get harder as time goes by."

"They will." Shayna stood in front of him. "What's this about redeeming Kasdeya?"

He cut a quick glance at Deema. "I just wondered if it were possible."

"It is, but not likely. Why?"

"It is?" He straightened. "There's something about her. I know she's evil, but she never fights. She's not once raised a hand to any of us. Why is that?"

"She isn't a fighter."

"I don't believe that. I think the heart of a warrior beats in her chest. I'd like to know who she was before becoming what she is now." He met her gaze with a sharp one.

"Don't let those thoughts keep you from putting your sword through her chest if it means her life or one of ours." With that, Shayna spun around and strode to the house.

Deema

"Stop thinking that way." Deema told Marshal. "Just because she can be redeemed, doesn't mean she will. Do you understand?"

"I do." He pushed away from the porch, eyes flashing, and strolled into the woods behind the house.

"What's more surprising than the news about Kasdeya is the softening of Marshal's heart," Payson said. "For him to worry so much about someone who's done the things Kasdeya has is nothing short of a miracle."

Deema stepped into his arms. "I don't understand his obsession with her."

"He sees something we don't. Marshal's always been perceptive. Don't discount his opinions."

She sighed. "I won't. Come, let's wash off the stench of battle." She took his hand and led him into the house, casting one last look to where Marshal had gone.

Once they'd all showered, changed clothes, and Marshal returned, tight-lipped about where he'd been, Agatha made coffee and they sat around the kitchen table. Deema sat, content to be silent, and dwelled on the face of all those she loved who sat there with her.

"Will your people be able to save the young man who got bit?" Agatha asked. "It was more than the graze he got."

A shadow passed over Shayna's eyes. "I hope so. It's his only chance."

"If they can't?" Pierce set his mug on the table.

"He'll be put to death in his sleep." A tear dripped down her cheek. "It's the best way."

Deema leaned over and put a hand on her arm. "It's part of battle. We all carry cuts and bruises." She rolled up her sleeve to show a purplish-blue mark the size of a baseball. If not for our armor, we'd all be in the same situation. What we need is protection for our necks."

"I agree." Payson glanced around the table. "The armor we wear protects everything but our neck. In the medieval days, they wore chain mail that hung down past their helmets. Is that possible?"

"I'll talk to Linette." Shayna pressed her hands on the table to stand.

The doorbell rang.

They all froze and stared at each other.

"What is that?" Deema asked.

"A doorbell, dummy. I read about one in a book." Agatha grinned and went to open the front door.

Mary Ann and four other women of varied ages stood there. "They all agreed to help," Mary Ann said. "Now, you've got an army."

"Five?" Agatha frowned. "That's not an army."

"I did say a handful." Mary Ann held up her hand, fingers spread.

Deema glanced at Payson. "A doorbell?"

"That's right. We've never had anyone come to the hotel or here before. A doorbell lets you know someone is at the door."

"Clever." In her world, they knocked. She eyed the witches with interest. A blond in her twenties, clearly the daughter of a woman in her forties. Another dark-haired woman around the same age, and another who looked close enough to Mary Ann to be her sister. Then Agatha, the oldest.

"Are all of you ancient?" Payson asked.

Mary Ann shook her head. "We chose the human world to hide in. We don't live longer lives here."

"Then you must return to The Glen when this is over," Deema said. "You'll be welcomed there."

"We've families here," one of them said. "That's another reason we choose to fight."

"Calm down." Mary Ann introduced them. "This sourpuss is my sister, Lisa. That's Becky and Sharon, mother and daughter. These two are Rachel and Lucille."

The men stood, giving up their chairs.

"I don't think it wise for you to go home once the enemy knows your face," Deema said. "It puts your families at risk. Do they know what you are?"

The witches glanced at each other. "No," Lisa said. "We only tell them if they show signs of magic. So far Becky is the only one."

"We'll tell them we need to go on a retreat," Mary Ann said. "I've done that before."

"That won't work." Deema glanced at Shayna. "You'll have to tell them, then take them to the safety of The Glen. That's the only place they'll be safe."

"Not necessarily," Pierce muttered.

"What?" Deema narrowed her eyes.

"The Glen will be under attack in a matter of days. We need to train these women and return there to protect them."

"What exactly will we be fighting?" Becky, the youngest asked. "I'm not married and have no children. I'm willing to come."

"Vampires and demons," Agatha grinned. "It's an adventure for sure."

Deema took a long deep breath. "We've seen Mary Ann fight. Where did you receive your training?"

"I was in the Army for twenty years. Fought in Afghanistan and took karate. My friends here won't know a sword from a butter knife."

"We start training as soon as you return from telling your families." Deema crossed her arms. "I won't step down from this decision. You either tell them and bring them to safety, or you don't fight with us."

Shayna nodded. "I agree. You cannot take the risk otherwise. Even under attack, they're safer in The Glen than here. Bring them to this house. We'll show them witches and faeries and dragons truly do exist."

"It's a real eye-opener if Shayna has to zap them," Pierce said with a laugh. "It definitely got my attention."

"Who's going to follow my orders and who isn't?" Deema eyed each of them.

The witches looked at each other, then Mary

Ann said, "We all will. See you here in a few hours with our families by our sides."

15
Deema

Before dusk, the families arrived. Looking shell-shocked, four husbands and three children ranging in age from ten to fifteen stared at those waiting on the front porch. Deema smiled. Poor humans. "How did you convince them?"

Mary Ann patted the face of a silver-haired man next to her. "We simply gathered them together and showed them what we could do. A bit of a shock, really. This is my husband, Frank. Meet the faeries, dear."

Pierce stepped forward. "We three are NYPD. It's good to meet you. You'll get used to the chaos." He thrust out his hand.

Frank returned the shake. "I'm retired Army. I'd like to fight."

"We're glad to have you." Deema studied the three children. "You three will stay somewhere safe with any of the others not fighting."

Mary Ann shook her head. "Frank, I'd rather know a man of your strength is protecting our families. Stay behind this time, dear."

"You're a faerie?" A sullen girl did her best to look bored and failed.

"Show them, Shayna." Deema would, but Shayna was the most impressive when in full armor. Getting their questions answered now would save time during training.

Shayna crossed her arms, brought them down hard at her sides and stood there in her bright blue, shining glory. She glanced at Pierce and laughed.

"Wow." The girl ran a hand down the suit. "What is this made of?"

"Dragon scales."

"Can we meet a dragon?" The oldest, a boy, asked.

"You'll meet a lot of creatures you thought only existed in books before this is finished." Mary Ann put a hand on his shoulder. "Oh, the things you'll see."

"Let's move them to The Glen, then start training in the morning." Deema whirled back to the house.

"Can we watch the training?" the boy asked. "There's time to leave later, right?" He glanced at Rachel. "Mom? We might pick up some pointers. What if the bad guys break through your ranks? We need to know how to defend ourselves."

She shrugged. "It's not up to me. These fierce ladies are in control now."

Deema stopped. "I see no harm in them

watching."

"Neither do I." Shayna changed back to her human clothes. "I'd rather keep them with us in case Alvar attacks sooner than planned. Tomorrow is time enough. Come. Let us find you a place to sleep."

The next morning, Deema woke to the noise of Agatha banging pans. She dressed and stepped over sleeping bodies on her way to the kitchen. "Are you trying to wake everyone up?"

"The more I think about it, the madder I get." She slammed her hands on the counter.

"Maybe I can help." Deema leaned her back against the refrigerator and faced the angry witch. "I can listen, at least."

Agatha took several deep breaths before speaking. "For years and years, I thought I was the last of my kind. Now, I find out I've padded around in front of one for a few months and she never said a word." She raised a red-rimmed gaze. "I'm both relieved and upset."

"These aren't the ones who would have left you alone in the woods. These have to be offspring of offspring. Don't be upset at them."

"Mary Ann knew what I was." She filled the sink with water.

"For her family's safety, she kept silent."

"You sound like Shayna, being all wise and consoling." Agatha added dish soap.

Deema laughed. "I'll take that as a compliment." She eyed the sudsy water. "Can't you clean the dishes with magic?"

"I can, but it relaxes me. When I'm finished, I'll

fix breakfast for this crowd and you can work them until they drop."

"They will definitely know they've been training when Shayna and I are finished with them." She pushed away from the fridge and stepped onto the front porch.

A slight breeze blew. Overhead three demons drifted, aimlessly searching for something they couldn't find. Now that she knew the light side had witches, Kasdeya would increase her efforts to locate their hiding place.

Deema clenched her fists to keep from shooting the demons out of the sky. Fighting could not happen close to the house and there wasn't time to lure them away and dispose of them. The sounds of those in the house waking pulled Deema back inside.

"No magic," she warned. "We've a few visitors floating around overhead."

The three children raced outside to see. Deema shook her head. Without their eyes opened, they'd have no idea what they were looking for. She'd leave that task to Shayna's discretion.

Agatha's mood hadn't improved much in the few minutes Deema was outside. She stood with crossed arms as Mary Ann tried to explain to her why she hadn't said who she was.

"I accepted the job at the precinct in order to be kept aware of the upcoming battle. My family has been neutral for so long, I wasn't sure I wanted to become part of the fight." She glanced at Frank. "Now, knowing what we're up against, I was right."

"You could have told me. We're the same, you

and I." Agatha wiggled her finger between them.

"My apologies." Mary Ann plopped in a nearby chair. "Still, what's done is done and we're here now. Swallow your pride and be glad."

"She's right." Deema joined her at the table. "We can't have division in our group. We have to depend on each of us. Let's fill our bellies and prepare to train."

"Can't do anything until Shayna returns with more swords." Agatha dumped a mound of scrambled eggs into a bowl. "She left before any of you were awake."

Shayna

Shayna followed Linette to the armory. "We need all that you can spare." She explained about the neck protection. "Not only weapons, but armor."

"It's good to know our side is growing. Our forge is working overtime to keep up with the needed weapons." Linette shoved open the heavy wooden door. "I trust Agatha will enchant the weapons?"

"Of course. Are things well here?"

"We've sent the children and non-fighters to the caves with the dragons. That's the safest place for them to be, even when war breaks out. There is room for your humans when they arrive." She held up a shining mesh. "Is this what you seek?"

Shayna grinned. "Yes. Is it possible to have production resume so every warrior has one? I blocked a vampire bite with my armor. We're hoping this will save our necks. How is the young warrior that Earin brought back?"

"Endured the painful cleansing of his blood and is recovering. It will take time to outfit everyone, but we'll work as fast as we can. You take the ones you need. Your small group is our first line of defense."

Shayna added ten of the twenty chain mail to a pile of armor on a table, and then turned to study the weapons hanging on the wall. The witches weren't as physically strong as either the faeries or the human men, having focused on magic. They needed something lethal, yet light. She added throwing knives to the pile, then five narrow swords. "With their magic, this should suit them well."

Linette nodded. "We are also training in the ways of fire. The information you brought about the demons' weakness is a great asset." She turned a grave look on Deema. "Alas, Alvar has resumed production of those monsters in the rooms below Brigette's castle. He is working on lessening their aversion to fire."

"That's not good news."

"No, but it keeps him too occupied to attack The Glen, and that is good news. We need all the time to prepare that we can get."

"We'll do our best to give you that time." Shayna put the weapons and armor into a crate and hefted it on her shoulders. "For as long as we can. There will come a time when we will have to bring the fight here in order to stop Alvar's forces."

"I know. But I fear the final battle will take place in the human world." She strolled from the room, blue robes trailing behind her.

Keeping a firm grip on the crate, Shayna headed for the portal. By the time she returned home, the others had eaten and waited impatiently for her arrival. She set the crate on the kitchen table. "I've everything we need." She pulled out the items.

"You got the addition to our armor." Pierce pulled her close in a one-armed hug.

"The blacksmiths will forge more. Our task for now is to keep the fight here in your world until ours is ready to face Alvar."

His features hardened, and he pulled away. "So, my people will keep dying while yours remain safe?"

Her heart pained. "We're doing our best to save as many as we can."

"Yet it's my world continuously at risk." He whirled and stormed away.

Shayna met Deema's worried gaze, then followed him outside. "What would you have me do? I'm following the orders of my queen. Keeping the dark in your city protects the rest of your country. If the darkness spreads, if the fae fall, if the humans fall, all will be lost. It has to end here. Ireland is fighting to keep Europe safe, I've heard tell of fighting in China. New York is where it's happening in America."

His shoulders slumped. "I know. Nothing is

ever fair in war, is it? And we are definitely at war."

She stood at his back and wrapped her arms around his waist, leaning into him. "We will train these witches and take the fight to Kasdeya. Once we rid your city of vampires, we can go to The Glen and stop Alvar. We will move from place to place ridding the world of darkness."

While the vampire force grew, the vampires still killed more than they converted. Their insatiable hunger made them unpredictable. Shayna needed to use their hunger against them. If only there was a way to make the people in New York's blood poisonous to the undead.

Pierce turned, being the one to hug her now. "What are you thinking?"

"Wishful thinking, actually. I wondered how to put enough silver into the city's water supply to kill vampires that feed on a person, yet not so much that the silver kills the person."

"You mean inject silver directly into the vampire's body."

She nodded. "It cannot be done."

"Instead of fighting the undead, why don't we carry syringes of liquid silver? The moment they get close enough, we inject them. That would definitely cut down on the amount we have to fight and kill them much faster."

She grabbed his face between her hands and kissed him. "You are a genius."

"Where are you going to get that much silver?" Agatha asked after Shayna presented the idea to the others.

"The Glen." She glanced at the others. "I think

it's an excellent idea."

"A time-consuming one. I can't enchant a syringe to return to the thrower like I can a knife. You'll have to get very close for it to work, and carry many."

"We wear armor so we can get close." Shayna refused to be dissuaded. Other than hand-to-hand combat, which tired the humans too quickly, this seemed the best alternative. "With Kasdeya's army growing here, and Alvar's growing in our world, we will face numbers too great to beat unless we cut them down at every opportunity."

Deema moved next to Shayna. "I think it will work. I'll head to The Glen and leave the training to Shayna. Where do we find these…syringes?

"I'll order them in bulk online," Pierce said. "You get the silver, I get the syringes, and our lovely Agatha will melt it to liquid form." He put an arm around her shoulder. "Still a team?"

Her cheeks reddened. "Of course, you silly man."

Shayna smiled. Pierce could always soften Agatha when no one else could.

16
Shayna

"Like this." Shayna showed the witches how to grip and swing their sword. "There will be no fancy footwork on the battlefield. It's swing and hack and jab. The undead and demons will not lessen their attack because you are tired or inexperienced. Your hand will grow slippery with perspiration, your arm weak with weariness. Still, you will fight until you have nothing more to give, then you will fight some more."

An arrow zipped past her head and imbedded in the center of a target Shayna had placed on a tree for knife throwing. She turned to see the teen girl on the porch, a crossbow in her hand.

"I'm a master at archery and had this in my bag," she said. "Call me Hanna the Fierce. You need me."

"No." Rachel shook her head. "You're only

fourteen. You will stay in the faerie city with the others."

"Dip my arrows in silver, and I won't have to get close to the enemy." Hanna stepped off the porch and stopped a foot away from Shayna. "You know my worth."

"I do. To shoot accurately from such a distance will help us greatly. You'll need armor."

"Nothing that impedes my aim. Is it possible to have pink?"

The girl's mother threw down her sword and stormed into the house. She returned a minute later with several arrows. She thrust them into her daughter's hand. "These belonged to an ancestor of mine. May they bring you luck." With a sad look in her eye, she kissed Hanna's cheek.

"Thanks, Mom. Will you enchant them for me?"

Still smiling, Shayna ordered the others to resume training. Pierce and the men had left early that morning for the city, leaving Shayna as the only one to spar with the witches. She went from woman to woman giving them tips and ignoring the complaints from the two boys as to why Hanna got to fight and they would have to hide like babies.

Agatha held out a plate of cookies, effectively silencing them, at least for the moment. "I'm too old to fight with anything but magic. Give it time. You, too, may get your chance in the future. The faerie city will need brave young men as you to protect its people."

Bless her. Cookies and kind words soothed hurt feelings.

After two hours, it became obvious that, other

than Mary Ann, the others might be more of hazard fighting than a help. "I think your magic would be used as our first wave of attack, then you all step back and let us take over." Even Becky lagged after a short time of brandishing her sword. There wasn't enough time to build up their strength.

"Then I say we pore over potions and spells," Agatha said. "With our minds, we'll cook up something magnificent."

What a grand thing if they came up with something to rid the world of all the undead at once. Foolish dreams. Shayna moved to the edge of the shield and peered out. The occasional car drove by. A woman walking her dog. Nothing out of the ordinary and no one seemed to sense the hidden house except the dog. When he tried to come that way, the woman tugged his leash and continued down the sidewalk. Life went on, oblivious to the danger lurking.

While Shayna no longer doubted her abilities as a warrior as she had when the war started, she still harbored a niggle of doubt as to whether the Light could win in the end. Things looked promising, but Alvar and Kasdeya were relentless.

She turned back to watch the witches and their family troop into the house. It was time to take the men and children to safety. All but the fiery Hanna, of course. The girl's ability with a bow was outstanding.

A cab stopped in front of the shield and Alvar's pet, Linc, got out. He sniffed and studied the area, his yellow eyes glowing.

Shayna gripped her sword, prepared to fight if

he pierced the shield. How had he found them?

Linc tilted its head and moved a few feet away, studying the grass on Shayna's side of the sidewalk. A cold smile stretched its lips. The dog glanced her way and saluted before returning to the cab.

Her gaze fell to the ground. Several sets of footprints in the mud where no house could be seen.

Shayna sheathed her sword and sprinted for the house. Bursting through the door, she said, "Gather your things. We must go now. Our location has been discovered."

"That darn hole Pierce put in the shield." Agatha started tossing things in her bag. "That's the only explanation. I didn't get it repaired in time. I'm sorry. I thought those things were too far away for it to matter."

"It isn't your fault. They were bound to find us sooner or later." Shayna threw weapons and armor back in the crate that now sat in the corner. It would take all her strength to teleport that many people, but none could be left behind for a second trip.

Agatha glanced out the window. "They're coming, and there's a lot."

"Grasp hands. Hold tight. Don't let go. You'll perish if you do." Shayna grabbed the hand of the youngest child. Agatha took hold of the hem of Shayna's coat, then the hand of Mary Ann. After making sure they were all connected, Shayna teleported, landing in front of the portal.

Her legs collapsed with the strain of moving that many bodies. Her head swam.

"Come on." Frank took the crate. "I won't go through that…tree without you. Your man would kill me."

Shayna glanced at his hand. "I'm unable." The sky darkened overhead. "You must go."

"Oh, no, you don't." Agatha grabbed her hand. "Take the other one, Frank. We'll drag her through." Her face paled as she looked up. "Right now. Let's go."

Shayna found herself half dragged, half staggering through the portal right before Linette sealed the entrance. "No. Pierce. The others." Shayna dropped to her knees. "They're alone now."

"Drink of the strengthening potion in your pocket and come with me." Linette marched away.

How could she after all the men had done for them? How could she close them off?

Deema stood next to her, tears shimmering in her eyes. "They're doomed. Without us, they'll die." Shayna lowered her head and sobbed.

Deema

Despite the pain ripping through her heart, Deema helped Shayna to her feet. "Come. Linette is expecting us." She swallowed past the lump in her throat.

"After all we'd done, after all we've gone through with them, how could she lock them out?"

"I don't know, but let's find out." Deema squared her shoulders. There would be another battle fought that day if the queen didn't have an explanation to satisfy a shattered heart.

The throne room echoed with shouts and faeries running to and fro. Deema paused in the doorway. She'd never seen the place so chaotic. "My queen?"

"Come." Linette ducked through a door on the other side of the room.

Deema and Shayna hurried after her.

The queen slid aside a secret panel and motioned them through. "There is little time to explain, but a scout has returned saying he overheard you'd been located. You arrived just in time. I closed the portal because you were followed. We cannot let the undead into our world. We have enough to deal with." She continued at a fast pace, coming out of the palace near an ancient tree. "This is a second portal. Go. Your men are under attack. You must make haste. Another sip of the potion, Shayna. You will need your strength."

"They can't attack the precinct," Deema said as Shayna followed the queen's orders.

"The men have been drawn out. A school is under siege. Go. Many lives are at stake. We've problems enough here. I will send help." With a swish of her robes, the queen rushed away.

If not for her love for Payson, Deema would have chosen to stay and protect her world. But now her heart lay somewhere else. She pushed aside a low-hanging branch and stepped into a cleft in the tree.

"Where are we?" They stood under a bridge.

Shayna shrugged. "I don't know this place." She placed a glowing palm on the concrete piling. "Now we can return to this spot." Grabbing Deema's hand, she teleported.

The men gathered around a SWAT vehicle in the parking lot of an elementary school. Pierce turned when Deema and Shayna appeared. "Thank God. We need you."

Payson's look was grave. "Three heavily armed men have taken the school. They don't respond to phone calls or the bull horn. There is no way in. All exits are locked."

"What do they want?" Deema moved to his side.

"No demands yet."

"It isn't the school they want, Payson." She turned him to face her. "You three have been drawn here to be killed. We've evacuated the others to The Glen. The park portal is closed."

"The witches?"

"At The Glen."

"We sure could use them right now. What do we do?"

Shayna cast a hedge of protection around them to prevent attack from the sky. "We wait until we see what we're up against."

"It won't be good," Deema said. "Whatever happens, Clark, know that I love you." She slipped her hand in his.

"Don't give up hope yet." He pulled her in for a kiss. "I love you more than you can ever know."

"Now may not be the proper time to say this, but if we survive the day, I choose to bind myself to you." She blinked back tears. "I should have done so long ago."

"Then, let's make sure we survive." He gave her a deeper kiss as the ground under their feet shook. "Because I'd like to marry you proper-like."

Her neck flushed. "Binding is the—"

"What is that?" Officer Charges took a few steps back, his face devoid of color.

At least fifty vampires stomped across the lot. There'd be no hiding what they were from the officers and SWAT team.

"Vampires," Pierce said.

"What?" Charges frowned. "You're serious?"

"Very." Pierce's face fell. "There is no way for you to fight them. Get inside the van." He turned to the SWAT team. "All of you."

"But, sir…" Charges shook his head.

"I've been trained to fight them. Go. Watch and learn. You'll need time to process what you're seeing. Shoot if you have an opening. Your bullets were switched to silver months ago."

The SWAT team hesitated until the vampires's eyes glowed red. A mad scramble to get inside caused the van to rock with the force of strong winds.

"We cannot beat them alone." Shayna squared her shoulders.

"But you can with us." Earin appeared next to them with all six witches and a frightened Hanna in tow. "Up there, love." He tossed the girl on top of the van. "Start shooting as soon as they are in range."

Rachel scrambled on top with her daughter, her

black hair flying around her face as she raised her hands.

As Hanna's arrows flew, so did bolts of fire from the witches' hands. Fire, then ice rained down on the now-charging undead. While Hanna's arrows hit their targets, and several fell under the onslaught from the witches, it was still a large group that converged on the fighters.

"Behind us," Deema ordered the witches. "It's up to us now. Keep your backs against the van and do not venture forth. Cast your spells only when there is no danger of hitting one of us."

Agatha turned into her dog form. Mary Ann clutched her sword. The others plastered their backs against the van and held out their hands, prepared to do magic if an opening presented itself.

"Hold steady." Deema stepped next to Payson as they faced their foe. "Change to armor." No sense in hiding who and what they were any longer. Too many eyes watched from the safety of the van.

Deema shot bolts from her fingers, her purple mixing with Shayna's blue. When the offenders reached within twenty feet, Shayna shot them with a bright light. They stumbled back but recovered, and advanced again. Deema gripped her sword and raised it overhead. With a sharp war cry, she sprinted toward the attackers with the cries of the others behind her.

17
Shayna

The vampires immediately went for the fighters' necks. Their fangs slid off the fine mesh of the neck armor with a scratching sound that sent shivers down Shayna's back. She thrust her sword forward, her weight on her right leg, putting all her strength into the jab. She'd no more than sent one undead to hell then another would attack until every breath was a jab, a slash, a swing of her blade.

Gunshots rang out from the van as those inside tried in vain to stop the horde from surrounding the fighters. Their erratic shots missed their targets more than they hit.

An arrow bounced off Shayna's armor. She cut a glance at Hanna, who shrugged and mouthed, "Sorry."

Pierce pressed his back against Shayna's. "They've reverted to their old ways of trying to separate us. Our circle has split into parts. The undead is working their way to the van."

"Fall back!" Shayna fought her way to the van, taking a stance in front of the witches. The others did the same, forming a half circle around the spell casters.

The vampires fell under shots fired at closer range. The air filled with black ash. Then, as fast as they'd attacked, the vampires retreated.

Shayna lowered her sword. Another skirmish won, but more would come. "We need to get inside the school."

Pierce motioned for the SWAT team. "We'll leave it up to them."

"Sir, I've never seen anything more frightening in my life." The SWAT leader stopped in front of the faes. "But I'm mighty grateful for whoever these people are." His gaze flicked to Agatha. "I recognize her from the bomber incident."

"She's a witch, and a mighty brave one. These two are faeries, along with the man with long hair. They'll lead the way into the building. Follow Agent Sky's lead while we stay behind and clean up here."

Shayna smiled and motioned to Deema and Earin. "Let's go." Fatigue coated the detectives and witches like the ash lingering in the air. Let them rest, Shayna thought.

Seven SWAT members followed as the faeries darted across the parking lot. Shayna stepped aside as one placed a small explosive on a side door. It opened with a muffled pop.

Shayna peered in, then entered first, Deema

next, then Earin. No one met them. No cries of alarm. No frightened office staff peering at them from behind glass. Dread rose in her chest.

"Where are they?" Deema whispered. "There should be crying children."

"I don't know." She headed down a hallway, peering in empty classrooms. She stopped in front of a set of double steel doors and pressed her ear against a small window covered with paper. Murmurs from the other side of the door reached her. "Inside."

Another explosive and the group rushed inside a cafeteria crowded with staff and students. The entire school had been packed inside the room, leaving many of them standing against the walls for lack of room.

Shayna glanced around. Where were the armed men?

A little girl tugged on the edge of her jacket. When Shayna glanced down, the child's eyes darted to the stage. Shayna motioned to the SWAT team to enter from the right. She took Deema and Earin with her to the left. Silent as spirits, the armor-clad law enforcement slipped through the side entrance.

The other three climbed a set of five stairs and entered behind a curtained backdrop. Three young men slumped against the back wall. Their hands, feet, and mouths duct-taped together. Confusion clouded their features. Next to them sat three sports bags.

Shayna pulled the tape from one of their mouths. "Explain."

"We were walking across the field on our way

to baseball practice," he said. "Some woman in red leather forced us to come inside. She said she'd kill us if we didn't do exactly what she said. She had a gun, so we believed her."

Shayna glanced at Deema's stern face. "Kasdeya."

"Then, she made us gather everyone in this room and pretend we had guns in our bags. Then, she tied us up and left."

Shayna jerked. The building had been locked up tight until they blew open the door. "She was still here when we arrived." She pushed to her feet. They'd been so close to capturing her. The demon would be long gone by now. "Cut them free." She radioed Pierce and the others that everything was fine and let them know who had been behind the distraction.

"We've got to stop her." Deema paced the stage. "The men we care about could have been killed today."

"Don't you find it strange that she didn't harm anyone here? The vampires could have massacred this school with little effort."

Deema stopped and faced her. "That's the reason Marshal holds onto the idea that Kasdeya can be changed. She hasn't killed anyone since this all started. She's following orders without doing any killing herself."

"To protect herself from Abaddon."

Deema

What if Marshal was right about Kasdeya? The only way to find out was to ask the demon outright. They couldn't do that unless they captured her. To do that, they needed to know her hiding place. The penthouse had been empty for days. Now, Deema sat in the police station while the men filled out reports and felt as useful as a wadded-up gum wrapper.

"We should be out there looking for her." Deema plopped into a chair in the bull pen.

"She seems to come to us often enough," Pierce said, glancing up from his computer. "Aren't you tired enough for one day? I'm beat."

She sighed. The only ones of their group not resting safely in The Glen were her, Shayna, and the three men. Pierce was behind locked doors with several of his uniformed officers explaining about what they were up against. Shayna made coffee. Always coffee with her, as if the drink solved the world's problems.

"You're in a bit of a mood." Payson reached across the desk and held her hand. "When we get home—"

"We cannot return to the house." Her gaze collided with his. "It's no longer safe."

"But…in The Glen…can we…?"

"I don't know." In her heart she knew the queen

would deny her request of binding to Clark until the war was finished. Here, in his world, it would have been too late by the time they moved to The Glen, and the deed done. The queen would tell her he was nothing more than a distraction.

She glanced over to where Shayna stood. She wanted Pierce as much as Deema wanted Clark, but the other faerie had the restraint to wait. Deema wasn't sure she did.

"I'd take you to a hotel," he said, "but I don't want it to be sordid. This is forever, you said. I want it to be special."

"Me too." She lowered her head.

Maybe Radella would know where Kasdeya hid. The demon was the key to ending it all. Find her, find Abaddon, and bind them both for eternity. "I shall return." She leaned over the desk and kissed him. "Soon."

He nodded, smiled, and returned to his reports.

Deema asked Shayna to go with her, and minutes later they stood in front of Radella.

The vampire sneered, looking exactly as she did the day they captured her. Being immortal, she'd not aged beyond the age she was when converted. "No longer queen? Pity."

"Hush." Deema squatted in front of her. "If Kasdeya isn't in her penthouse, where would she be?"

"Why would I tell you?"

"Because my knife is covered with silver." Deema grinned. "With Shayna no longer queen, she can't forbid me not to torture you."

Radella's gaze flicked to Shayna, then back to

Deema. "She's most likely with Alvar."

"No, he's in our world. There's been no sign of her here."

"Then, I don't know."

"You lie." Deema pulled her knife.

"I'm not." The vampire's eyes widened. "I worked for her. We weren't confidants."

"She has someone else converting now in large numbers," Shayna said. "Who?"

"The bouncer from the club, same as before. With his size and strength, resisting would be futile."

Deema smiled and stood. "You've been helpful. Perhaps, soon, we'll send you to your eternal fate." The vampire hissed as the faeries strolled away.

"What did you learn?" Shayna asked, as they headed for the throne room.

"That Kasdeya is most likely with Dan, I think that was his name. We find him, we find her. He must have had a dwelling place before Radella sank her teeth into him." Clark would know how to find him. "I need to speak with our queen. Will you wait for me?"

Although she knew the answer, she still needed to make the request. Queen Linette sat on her throne while her subjects lined up to speak with her. Her eyes lit up at the sight of Deema. "Come forward. You have no time to wait in line."

Deema approached the throne as irritated faeries watched. She bowed. "My request is a private one and nothing to do with fighting."

"Then come. Let's retire to my chambers." Linette practically floated from her throne. "I am in need of refreshments." Once inside, she closed the doors. "I heard of the incident in front of the school. A job well done. Unfortunately, more and more humans become aware of the fae world."

"It couldn't be helped. We need them at this time." She folded her hands in front of her. "I've come to ask your blessing on Clark Payson and me binding."

Linette poured a crystal goblet full of water. "You can only bind to one in your lifetime. What if he should perish in this war?"

"Then I will remain alone for however many years I have left." She raised her head and met Linette's concerned gaze.

"I cannot allow it. You may not realize the ramifications of doing this at such a time, but I do." Sadness flickered across her features. "I too once loved, way before I became queen. He was killed, and now I must be alone. My heart has never recovered."

"Change the law." Deema's voice shook. "You are the queen. Let us love who and when we want. Some of my years will pass to Clark. I won't have as long to live if he should die, and I gladly accept my fate."

Linette shook her head. "You will be so concentrated on protecting him that you will lose focus in a battle. I cannot bless your union at this time. Fetch the others and return to The Glen. The darkness grows, and Alvar advances."

18
Shayna

"I can't go." Pierce stepped back from her embrace. "I'm the chief of police. I cannot leave my city unprotected. You are needed here more than in The Glen. Why must your queen always put the faeries first? Your fate depends on our survival."

"My place is with my people. The queen has ordered us to return." Shayna forced the words from a tortured throat. How will she fight knowing Pierce was in constant danger in his world? "You vowed to love me."

"I do love you, with every fiber of my being." He pulled her back into his arms. "But I must stay for the very reason you must go." He cupped her face and stared into her eyes. "You are the light in my heart, the hope that keeps me fighting. When Alvar attacks, I will come. Until then, I am needed here."

"I cannot protect you." The tears escaped and ran down her cheeks. At that moment, she was not a warrior, but a woman who's heart shattered piece by pierce to be crushed under a boot. "If you're attacked by another horde—"

"SWAT will protect me. They have shields, protective gear, and silver bullets. I have my armor." He leaned his forehead against hers. "We have to trust it will be enough. We feared this day would come, Shayna. We will survive it to have a future together."

She nodded. "I will have faith." Before her tears could turn into sobs, she spun around and rushed from his office.

The receptionist desk sat empty with Mary Ann in The Glen. Shayna joined the waiting Deema and clutched her hand. "This is a sad day."

Deema nodded, her face streaked with tears. "We shall see them again."

With one last glance over her shoulder, Shayna locked gazes with Pierce, and teleported back to The Glen. She stood outside the portal and fought to regain her composure. As a trained warrior, she wasn't supposed to fall in love. Love made one lose the focus necessary to fight. She understood the queen's order they return, but she didn't have to like it.

She squared her shoulders and lifted her head. She would do what needed doing, then see Pierce again. Somehow, she needed to convince him to come to The Glen where he would be safe

"I have the address for Radella's former

bouncer." Deema waved a slip of paper. "I'd like to check it out at the first opportunity."

"And we will." Together they headed for the throne room, standing in front of their queen like stoic bookends.

Linette sighed. "I rule as I deem necessary. It will do you no good to pout. I need you to scout out Alvar's army. Gorna and Dragona are waiting for you in the courtyard. Do not be captured." Her light blue eyes glittered like sapphires. "I have no one else to send but my best warriors. Return by nightfall."

Things were bad. The queen had never been this curt before. Shayna bowed and backed from the room. "She's gravely worried."

"I got that feeling, too. On dragons, we won't be able to get close to Alvar without being seen."

"Use the dragons." Brigette stepped from behind them. "Raze the city. I will rebuild. We cannot allow him to keep making those…things."

"Are you sure?" Shayna studied the queen's impassive face. "There will be no going back. You can't pull us away in the middle of the destruction."

"I understand." She strode away, flanked by guards.

"My heart aches for her people," Deema said.

"Our people now. We are one." Shayna led the way to the courtyard. "We are to destroy the Circle of Mushrooms," she told Gorna. "Call the others."

Gorna blinked. "On whose orders?"

"Queen Brigette. Destroy the city and the demon army." Shayna leaped onto her back as Deema did the same on Dragona. "Have them meet us in Poppy Field."

Gorna roared, spewed fire, and rose into the sky. "These are frightening days."

"Yes, my friend, they are." Shayna lay against her neck and scanned the ground below them. "Be careful not to be seen. We don't have time for a battle."

"I understand." Gorna rose higher, using the clouds as cover until they reached the field of poppies. She landed softly on the ground. "The others are coming."

Shayna glanced up as dragons soared from the clouds. If she wasn't a friend of the beasts, she'd cower in fear. She stood on Gorna's back. "We are not to leave any of the city. It must all be destroyed and as much of Alvar's army as possible."

"Feel free to kill Alvar," Deema added.

Shayna laughed. "Anyone on the dark side must be extinguished. Stay high, be careful, and make haste when the job is done."

As if one body, the dragons roared and rose with mighty flaps of their wings. Gorna and Dragona took the lead.

As they drew closer, Shayna's blood ran cold. Things were worse than she'd thought. There was no way they'd get out without a fight.

Tens of thousands of demons roamed the area around the city. Destruction without being seen would be near impossible. She stuck out her arm, and Gorna plummeted, lying a wide path of fire down the center of the city. A thick cloud of demons rose to attack.

Dragona followed in Gorna's path cutting the

group of demons in half. Still more came until the air filled, and the dragons couldn't fire without hitting each other.

"Concentrate on the city!" Shayna took the silver rope from her belt and tied herself firmly to Gorna's back. "Deema and I will do what we can to distract the horde." She raised her hands and shot out a bolt of light, then another and another, until her palms burned. Still the demons came.

From underneath the burning city more demons, thick as flies, appeared from the underground rooms. Shayna leaned forward. "Destroy the rooms below."

Gorna swooped and bellowed fire.

Shayna held tight to her neck, making herself as small a target as possible. A demon landed in back of her. Before she could turn, it raked its claws down her back, cutting through the armor and into her flesh. Shayna screamed and fell, hanging off the dragon's back as her chain kept her from plummeting to her death.

Gorna turned her great head and burned the demon to a crisp, then dove under Shayna, lifting her to safety. "The city will burn. There is no putting out the fire until it is spent. We must get you back to The Glen."

"We need to rid this world of as many demons as possible."

"You'll die if we stay. It's time to go." Gorna stayed low and fast until they reached the courtyard. "Even now, your legs tremble."

Dragona landed with an unconscious and bloody Deema clutched in one claw. "She barely breathes."

Earin and another faerie rushed forward. "We've got them now. Tend to your own wounds. We owe you a debt of gratitude."

Shayna peered into Earin's face as she fell into his outstretched arms and let the blackness take over as she whispered Pierce's name.

Deema

Deema woke screaming. Her leg burned as if the very fire of Hades raged under her skin.

"Here you go." Nurse Zina applied a cooling salve. "This is not the same poison used before. It took some effort to create an antidote."

"Alvar has created a demon whose claws cut through dragon scales and drip acid." Queen Linette entered the room. "One of the dragons was able to capture one. It is bound in the dungeon."

"I will come." Deema attempted to rise.

"No, my brave warrior." Linette put a hand on her shoulder, gently pushing her back. "You have healing to do."

"Shayna?"

"I'm here." Shayna's spoke from the next bed, her voice as weak as Deema felt. "Barely."

"How will we fight them if our armor doesn't stand up against their attack?" Deema faced her friend.

"We have the witches working on something," Linette said. "Worry not. This is an obstacle we can overcome."

"The demon numbers are great, my queen." Deema struggled to a sitting position as the nurse plumped pillows behind her. "Is there hope that Alvar has been killed?"

Linette shook her head. "One of the dragons saw him escape, riding on the back of one of the creatures he created. At least for now, the promise of an imminent attack has been diverted. You did well. I will check on you later."

It was good the men had not been with them. They couldn't have lived through the attack. How would they be kept safe when the final battle came?

"I see the worry on your face," Shayna said. "I share the feeling. I would have lost Pierce today foever."

"Agatha and the others will think of something." Deema gritted her teeth against the incessant burning and closed her eyes.

She woke to someone smoothing the hair back from her face. A soft kiss on her lips. "Clark."

"I like that you've taken to calling me by my first name." He smiled down at her. "Earin came and told us you'd been injured."

"For that I am grateful." She clutched his hand. "The queen didn't give her blessing to bind."

He gave a sad smile and rubbed his thumb across the back of her hand. "She told me and of her reason why. We'll wait. I'm not going anywhere." He raised her hand to his lips. "You scared me, my beautiful warrior. I wish you and Shayna wouldn't go out without an army by your side."

"I'm sorry. How are things in your world?"

"Growing darker at an alarming rate." He glanced to where Pierce sat next to Shayna's bed. "There isn't a lot we can do. I feel split in two, wanting to be here with you, and knowing I have to be there with my people. I'm not a warrior, Deema. I'm a man who happens to have had a very good trainer in the art of warfare."

"You're losing faith?"

"Sometimes I feel as if my faith is far away." He raised a tortured gaze. "If I lose you, there's no point in saving any world."

"If I should fall, if you should fall, the other will follow. That's how big is my love for you." She blinked back tears. "To think I almost never met you. How foolish was I to follow the dark."

"Pretty foolish." He grinned.

She laughed. "Let's talk no more of dark things. Have you eaten?"

"No, but I'll make sure to eat before heading back. You know how much I like the food here." He straightened, tucking her hand against her side. "You rest. I'll be back tomorrow. I can't go a day without seeing your face."

"Nor I yours." She watched as the men left, then turned to Shayna. "We cannot fight a war in two worlds and expect to win."

"I know. We need to draw one into the other. The problem is which world do we center the war in?"

"The human one. Here, an entire race can be

wiped out with one battle. There, only a city."

"If we lose, the darkness spreads to the rest of the world."

"Giving the people time to fight." Deema sighed. "There is no perfect solution, only which bad choice is the best." How would they get Alvar to leave The Glen alone and move back to the human world? What could they use to lure the traitor? What did Alvar treasure most in all the worlds? Himself.

Deema studied every option and came to no conclusion. Since the fae treasured only himself and power, he could only be lured with the promise of more power. "We need something to use as bait. Something to lure Alvar into a trap, making him think he'll be stronger if he possesses it. Whatever it will be."

"That's a good plan." Shayna propped herself on one elbow. "Something that will make him think he can spy on us and know our every move before we make it." She grinned.

Deema met her grin. "Agatha's crystal ball."

19
Shayna

Three days after the demon attack and, still bearing the scars on her back, Shayna approached the tower where the witches brewed their magic and concocted spells. The thick stone door slid on well-oiled hinges as she pushed it open.

Six heads bent over a large table where open books lay. "We're busy," Agatha said. "I hope this is important, otherwise go away. We're trying to find a way to keep your armor from being shredded."

"That's good to know, but I need your crystal ball." Shayna paused in the doorway.

"Okay, you have my attention." The old woman straightened and crossed her arms.

"I need you to enchant the ball so that if Alvar looks into it, he sees us but not our real actions. He needs to be fooled, except for the time and place of the final battle. We're hoping to use the ball to lure him. We need to face his forces in one world, not two. Can it be done?"

Agatha tilted her head. "Yes, but it's the only ball I possess. Once lost, it's gone forever."

"Can you spare it?" Shayna had no more ideas.

"I can, but I'll grieve its passing. When do you want it finished?"

"As soon as possible." She moved forward and put a hand on her friend's shoulder. "I appreciate the sacrifice and will do everything in my power to get the ball back to you."

Agatha shrugged. "Sacrifices are made in war. Better a crystal ball than a life. It will be ready in the morning."

"Thank you." Shayna left, closing the door behind her and went in search of Deema. She found her in the armory studying the weapons hanging on the wall. "Which of these is best at getting information from a demon without actually killing it?"

"Interrogating today?"

Deema nodded. "I don't want to make the wrong choice and ruin our chances at information."

"Choose nothing with silver or holy water, but you can most likely threaten with the water." Shayna pressed her lips together. "Of course, the ruse is up if he challenges you to cut him."

Deema sighed and chose a jewel-handled dagger. "I've always fancied this one."

"Good. I'm ready when you are." Shayna spun to lead the way to the dungeon.

Hanna darted up to them as they passed the gardens. "Hold up, please. I've a question."

Shayna raised her eyebrows.

"I know we'll be fighting soon, and I received my sparkling pink armor, but I really need more arrows. I retrieved the others after the demons blew away, you know, their ashes and all, but if I had a never-ending quiver…"

Shayna glanced at Deema. "I've never heard of such a thing."

"Neither have I. The child is dreaming. We'd all love never-ending weapons."

Hanna frowned. "Well, Pierce's knives return to him after he throws them."

"Do you really want your arrows zipping back at you?" Shayna chuckled. "No, we'll just make sure you have plenty and that your aim is true."

"Can I shoot from the back of a dragon? That would be cool."

Shayna glanced in the direction they'd been going. While she enjoyed the young girl's company and wild ideas, time was not something they had a lot of. "My suggestion is you visit your mother and see what she and the others can do to help you. We must be going."

"Ugh. No one has time for me." The girl stormed away.

"Queen Linette has requested you to come to the throne room immediately," a passing guard said.

Would they never be able to interrogate the demon? Shayna took a deep breath to calm her rising irritation and followed the guard.

The throne room was empty save for the two queens and a small table. Two parchments lay on the table next to a quill and bottle of ink.

"Good, you've arrived." Queen Linette waved them over. "We need your signatures. Shayna's here, Deema's there."

"What is this?" Shayna scanned the paper, her heart plummeting to her knees.

"If something happens to me in the battle, you are to take my place." Linette handed her the quill. "Deema will reign at your side in Brigette's place."

"And if we perish?"

"Then the throne reverts to the next in line. Earin. You know we will be targeted when the fight begins, just as last time."

"I did not enjoy being queen." Shayna shook her head. "Bypass me and go straight to Earin."

"He is the last resort. Our people have always been ruled by a woman." She shoved the quill closer, her eyes flashing. "Are you disobeying a direct order?"

"No." To do so would mean death. She took the quill. "Let it be known I sign under duress. The better idea would be for you to stay safely in The Glen until this is won."

"A queen always fights at her people's side. I will be no different."

Shayna closed her eyes in acceptance and signed the parchment before handing the quill to Deema.

Deema

Deema raised her gaze to meet the sad one of Shayna. "Why me? I'm from lowly stock."

"You are the best warrior our people have, and still of our bloodline." Brigette smiled. "I can think of no one better to rule in my place." She motioned her head to the parchment. "If you will, please. We've other matters to take care of."

Her hand shook as she signed. If Brigette perished, Deema could never be with Clark. The queen had to live at all costs.

"Don't die," Shayna told them, "because if I rule again, the first thing I will do is change the silly law of a queen not having a mate or giving her blessing for two people to love each other." She turned and marched from the throne room.

Deema grinned. "I like that idea." With one last look at the serious faces of the queens, she hurried to catch up with Shayna. "You've gone from a devoted and obedient servant to one who speaks her mind with no regard of the circumstances. Well done."

"There is no humor in this. I am still obedient, or I would not have signed the parchment."

"Regardless, I really like the new Shayna." Deema shoved open the door to the dungeon. "After you, oh temperamental one."

The corner of Shayna's mouth twitched. "Hush.

We've serious business ahead of us and must be stern."

Their boots echoed on the marble floor as they made their way to where Radella and the demon were held. The vampire had scooted as far from the demon as her chains would allow, which put her just out of the creatures reach. The demon squatted in the center of a circle drawn with holy water and glared at their approach.

"Get me out of here," Radella ordered. "He reeks of death and decay."

"You're one to talk." Deema passed her and stopped in front of the demon.

He lunged, stopping at the edge of the circle, his clawless hands hanging at his sides. "How are you alive? It was me who slashed your leg."

"Then I have a debt to pay you." Deema clutched the dagger, pulling it from its sheath. "Answer my questions, and I might spare you."

"Why does the light-colored one not speak? She's the leader." His gravelly voice caused the hair on her arms to rise. "We all know who the true warrior is."

"Let me tell who I am. I'm the enforcer. I enjoy doing the dirty work. Who clipped your claws?"

He spit at her feet. "Release me."

"Where is Alvar?"

"Release me."

Deema removed a bottle of holy water from her pocket and poured it over the blade of the dagger. "Where did he flee to?"

The creature's eyes widened, and he scurried back. "Away."

She exhaled slowly. "To where?" She took a step forward.

"Careful," Shayna whispered. "He is full of deceit and malice."

"I am deceit and malice," the demon sneered. "Alvar is again in the human world with all of his creations becoming stronger and more deadly than you can know."

"Where?" Deema held the knife close to the creature's throat. "The world is a big place."

"The mountains above the city under attack."

Deema glanced up at Shayna. "Will Pierce know of the place he speaks?"

"Perhaps."

"Shall I kill him?"

Shayna shook her head. "We will wait and make sure he is telling the truth, if he's capable of doing so. Come. We've other places to be."

"Wait." Radella strained against her chains. "Finish me, I beg you. Don't keep me here for eternity."

"We may still have need of you. Rest assured," Shayna said, "we will send you to your fate when the war is done."

"What if you lose?"

"Then you'll be stuck here forever." Deema flashed a grin and followed Shayna from the dungeon. "Do you think Alvar is in New York?"

"No. He will have chosen a place close, but further away to avoid easy detection. I do believe he is somewhere surrounding New York, though. Where his creations won't be affected by fire."

"The ocean?" Deema's steps faltered. "If he

takes the battle there, only those who fly can fight. That cuts our numbers dramatically."

"Another reason to lure him to where we want him. I doubt he'll fight over water. The vampires cannot fly. It's time to pay a visit to vampire Dan."

"We need a plan."

"I'm working on one." Shayna headed for the portal. "The ball will not be ready until morning. We need to find this undead and also a place to hide the ball where it will be found by Alvar or Kasdeya, and not an unsuspecting human."

Deema ducked into the portal behind her. "We need to know where the ball is at all times. A tracker."

"It will have one. Trust me. I've thought it through." Shayna scrunched her nose. "The men know this city better than we do. Let's seek their advice."

They teleported to the precinct, intercepting a fast food delivery of pizza. As much as the detectives loved faerie food, the faeries loved pizza. "Anyone hungry?" Deema set the box in the center of the table in the breakroom.

"For you." Clark nuzzled her neck. "I wasn't expecting you this early."

"We need your help." Deema opened the box and grabbed a slice, inhaling the mouth-watering aroma of cheese, tomatoes, and pepperoni. She ate as Shayna explained about Dan and the crystal ball.

"You want a large area with few inhabitants." Pierce rubbed his chin. "Perhaps the Town of Tahawus in the Adirondack mountains will work. It's an entirely abandoned town with iron mines and thick woods."

Deema glanced at Shayna. Could they be that lucky? "It sounds exactly like the place the demon had spoken of. Perhaps he told the truth after all." Iron bound the fae. It was the perfect place. "How would Alvar get past the faeries' aversion to iron?"

"Just as important is how will we get past ours?" Shayna fell back into a rolling chair, coming to a stop at the opposite wall. "It really is the perfect place for him to hide if he found a way."

Deema reached for a napkin. "Sounds like another job for the witches."

Clark leaned his elbows on the table and glanced from face to face. "Let us check it out first. If he's there, then you can worry about how to get past the iron."

"If Alvar finds a way past the iron, he may very well find a way to protect himself from lemon juice," Pierce said.

Deema's blood chilled. "Nevertheless, Shayna and I will go with you."

20
Shayna

"There is no way to get you past the iron."

Agatha shook her head. "Alvar cannot be in the mines, but his demons can. No, you'll find that traitor above ground." She handed Shayna a black velvet box. "Hide this somewhere away from that ghost town. The Grand Canyon in Arizona maybe or that mountaintop in Asia, or the place where we fought in Montana. Just not where you'll be stopped by iron."

"I'm not an imbecile." Shayna smiled to take the edge off her words. "We'll hide this and pay a visit to the vampire while the men scout out the vacant town. Can you protect us from lemon juice?"

"We can enchant your armor, but if a drop touches your skin…"

"We'll be careful. Thank you. We couldn't do any of this without you." She hurried to where

Deema waited. Explaining Agatha's theories, they ducked through the portal.

"Where have you decided to put this?" Deema pointed to the box.

"Central Park. I want Alvar to find it. The only true information he'll receive when he looks into it is that we're gathering our forces again on the mountain range in Montana. We've fought and won a battle there once, so perhaps the Light would help us do so again."

"Has anyone heard from Seamus recently about the situation in Ireland?"

"No, we've been too busy here. All I know is that he'll come with his followers when we fight, whether it be today or in the coming weeks. He has the situation under control." She teleported them to Central Park and hid the box under a thick bush near where the portal to The Glen had once been. She cast a shield over it to prevent human eyes from discovering the box. "Let's go talk to this Dan."

Deema read aloud the address and Shayna teleported them to a rundown motel renovated into small apartments. "Wow. You'd think someone killing and robbing the way he does would find somewhere nicer."

"It's just a place to sleep." She glanced around the parking lot full of potholes, the sign hanging lopsided from wires that no longer worked, and the faded salmon paint on the concrete walls. Deema was right. A person would think he'd find a nicer place.

Should they knock? Break down the door? Call out his name? She'd never confronted a vampire before that she didn't intend to kill. The scuff of a shoe gave her pause. She put a finger to her lips and motioned her head in the direction the sound had come from. "We mustn't let Alvar find the crystal ball near the old portal. If he does, he'll know every move we make. The darkness will have a stronghold."

Deema nodded, catching Shayna's silent message. "Then let's rid the world of his spawn before that happens, starting with the one behind this door."

"Looking for me?" Dan stepped around the corner, slapping an iron rod in the palm of his left hand. "I hoped to have my dinner delivered, and then here you are."

Shayna pressed one hand on her sword. The man stood well over six feet, putting him several inches taller than her. Although she could take him, she took a step back and gripped Deema's hand, teleporting them to the precinct as Dan leaped.

"Bait delivered to the idiot vampire," Deema announced the moment they stepped into the bull pen. "Your turn to make sure he tells Alvar."

"How are we supposed to do that?" Pierce grabbed his coat. "We can let you know whether the faerie is there, but to make a vampire the size of Dan do anything is out of my scope of ability."

"Wrong choice of words." Shayna leaned in the doorway. "Better said would be for you to let us know if he does. We'll go with you, but we can't enter the mines if that's where Dan goes."

"Alvar won't be there. He'll be hunkered down in a house somewhere." Pierce planted a kiss on her cheek as he passed. "Let's go, folks. Daylight is wasting."

Pierce slid into the driver's seat of a van the color of pea soup. "I know this thing sticks out like a sore green thumb, but it's the only thing that will hold all of us. If we get caught, we can't tell Alvar we teleported. Then, he'll know the two of you are here."

Marshal tapped him on the head. "Good thinking, boss. We'll just announce ourselves on the way with an engine that knocks."

"I agree with Pierce." Shayna climbed in the front passenger seat. "We'll stop far enough away so they can't see us. You'll need a viable explanation if questioned."

"Of course, you'd agree with him." Marshal clicked his seatbelt into place.

"What's gotten into you?" Payson scowled.

"Nothing. Just ready for this all to be over so life can get back to normal."

"It'll never be back to what it was before." Pierce turned the key in the ignition.

The sun sat high in the sky by the time Pierce pulled off to the side of the road. Shayna motioned for everyone to stay in the car until she deemed everything safe. She stood in the midst of the trees and listened to the breeze through the branches. The sun shimmered through leaves dappling the ground with gold. A bird twittered somewhere overhead. No sense of danger came to her, though she knew it lurked, waiting to catch them unaware.

She closed her eyes and raised her face heavenward. If only she could bask in the sunshine.

But no, rest was not an indulgence she could afford. Not as long as Abaddon hid behind Alvar and Kasdeya. "It's clear."

The others piled from the vehicle and checked their weapons before setting off down the road. While Shayna and Deema stayed in the shadows out of sight, the men approached the rotting wooden buildings, which grass and weeds were quickly reclaiming.

"Go in the Light," Shayna whispered as Pierce, flanked by the other two disappeared over a hill.

Deema

"I can't stay here in hiding. Our men are entering the devil's den. We can at least watch from the protection of the forest in case they encounter danger." Deema moved forward.

"We can't be seen unless it cannot be avoided." Shayna held back a low-lying branch. "At the first feel of iron freezing you into place, you must retreat. We cannot be captured."

"Only if Clark doesn't need me will I stay hidden." Deema was finished with rules and orders designed to keep her from the man she loved. "Can you really step aside if Pierce is in trouble?"

"No," Shayna said softly. "I would step in front

of death for him."

"You might have to before this is over." Silence screamed across the road. No sound of movement, voices, animals. Even the breeze ceased to blow the closer they got to the abandoned town. Evil did indeed inhabit the place.

They passed a two-story wooden home with a sagging porch. Several other once-occupied homes could barely be seen through thick foliage overgrowing the dwellings. In the distance rose the abandoned mine works. Circling a tower like bats were several demons.

Shayna and Deema caught up to the men and hunkered down behind an abandoned wagon. "We're assessing the situation before continuing," Clark said. "There's no way to get closer without those demons seeing us."

"You'd have to go through the buildings and fight your way through the woods," Deema said. "Go slow and quiet. You'll get close before you're seen. Follow me."

Keeping low and watching every placement of her feet, Deema led them closer to the large buildings ahead of them. A rushing creek on their left hid the sounds they made as they moved. She kept her gaze locked on the circling demons and stopped in front of a partially-boarded mine shaft. "I don't feel any iron," she whispered. "Shouldn't we?"

Shayna's features stiffened. "He's found a way to erase the effects, maybe. A charm?"

"Or the mining went very deep," Pierce said. "It's too dangerous for the two of you to go any further. We'll be back as soon as we catch a glimpse of Alvar or Dan."

"What about Linc? Don't you want to see me?" The jaguar snarled from behind them and leaped.

Deema threw herself in front of Clark and raised her sword. Not having the same strength in its claws as the demons, the cat's scratch was nothing more than an annoyance. Her sword pierced the shifter through the gut.

Shayna swung her sword and severed its head. "So much for secrecy. Get ready to fight." She turned as the demons who had once circled the tower darted toward them.

Alvar stepped onto the porch of one of the less dilapidated buildings and shouted for the demons to return to their post. He then spoke to someone still in the house.

Dan and two other vampires, all holding swords of iron, advanced upon the group. As they crossed the street, Dan grinned. "Party time."

"We have to go." Deema whirled and led the group crashing through the trees. They reached the edge of the creek, clutched hands, and teleported to the van. She glanced back as they sped away to see the undead left standing in the middle of the gravel road. Three large wolves sat next to them. Alvar no longer had an intolerance to iron and now armed his undead army with the very thing that kept the faeries at bay. He'd also found a pack of shifters.

She rested her head against the seatback. "If he finds a way to tolerate lemon juice, we're doomed."

"I think that answers our question as to whether or not the vampire contacted the faerie." Marshal gave a cheeky grin. "So now what?"

"We gather in The Glen's throne room and cook up some fake information to send the man running to the wrong place. At first, he'll send small groups of fighters out to attack. Eventually, we hope to draw him to a place where he can be captured or killed. Then Kasdeya will have to make her presence more known. After her, there's no one standing in front of Abaddon." Shayna glanced into the back seat. "He's our primary target. Binding him has to be the ultimate goal."

"Why not just kill him?" Marshal leaned forward. "Draw him out and kill him. Heck, I'd be happy to do the deed."

"He's the leader of the undead," Deema said. "He cannot die."

"Great. We've got something akin to Satan himself that we have to get close to and bind with chains. We're all going to die."

"No, we aren't." Pierce slowed their speed once they reached the freeway. "Positive thinking only. We've managed to stay one step ahead of the darkness. I don't see why that would stop. We have an army of magical beings. The dark only has Alvar and has to rely on brute strength. The man looked as if he's aged a century since we saw him last. The fight is definitely taking a toll."

Deema agreed. Once, the only sign of advancing age had been the faerie's silver hair. Now wrinkles lined his face and his shoulders bowed. She smiled. All the extra magic he'd been forced to use in order to keep himself safe could well be the thing that caused his demise.

21
Shayna

Linette shook her head and held a finger to her lips as soon as Shayna and the others entered the throne room, then led them to her private chambers. Once inside, she bolted the doors. "It's imperative no one hear us. This is the only secure room in the palace, safe from what Alvar might see or hear through the crystal ball."

"What is it?" Shayna studied the face of her queen, noting the worry lines on her once-smooth forehead. Alvar wasn't the only one showing signs of stress from the war.

"Hanna has gone through the portal into the human world." She handed over a note. "She said she's going to capture Kasdeya."

Shayna's eyes widened. "The child knows where the demon is hiding?"

"Impossible," Deema said. "How can she know

what we don't?"

"Regardless, the child is gone." Linette dropped onto her bed. "Understandably, her mother is distraught."

"We will find her." Shayna turned to leave.

"How?" Linette's worried tone stopped her. "We cannot jeopardize the lives of many for one wayward child."

Shayna narrowed her eyes. "We can't let her perish. Her skill with the bow is unparalleled." She would not back down. The girl must be saved. "Rachel?"

"Guarded in the tower by the others. We cannot lose her, either."

"It sounds as if you've given up on the girl, my queen." Shayna knelt in front of her. "I will risk the punishment of disobeying you, but we must find her before Kasdeya does. The girl was seen by the undead when we fought at the school. She is not a secret."

The queen waved a hand. "Go. You have one day. You must return by morning with or without her."

With a quick glance at Deema, Shayna raced for the Portal, the other faerie on her heels. Once through, they headed straight for the precinct to enlist the men's help.

Pierce paled. "She's wandering the city alone?"

"She won't survive," Marshal said. "The vampires are patrolling in greater numbers." He stood and grabbed his shoulder holster.

"Slow down." Pierce held up his hands. "We can't run out there willy-nilly. She could be anywhere. This is New York, not The Glen."

Shayna paced. "She could be injured, dying. We can't sit here."

"We won't." Pierce stood. "Most of the vampire activity has been focused around Harlem. This may be the city that never sleeps, but we've enforced a curfew. Some areas refuse to follow the order and are paying the ultimate price with their lives." He held out his hand. "Take us there, Shayna."

They teleported to the corner of ninety-sixth street. A few faces peered at them from barred windows. A few doors slammed.

"This isn't good," Marshal said. "Not even the hookers are out."

"If you see any movement at all," Shayna said, "interrogate. If it's a follower of the dark, kill it." She withdrew her sword. Hanna could be anywhere. "If you can get a human to talk, ask if they've seen her. She couldn't have disappeared without a trace." How she hoped Rachel hadn't turned. If she was, she would lose all hope, right along with most of the inhabitants of The Glen.

Keeping to the shadows, they scoured the alleyways for signs of the girl. It truly did seem as if she'd disappeared.

Shayna swiped the back of her hand across her eyes, smearing tears. Warrior, ha. A missing human girl with a stubborn streak reduced a so-called warrior to a frightened, blubbering mess.

"We'll find her." Pierce put his arms around her.

"Promise?" She gave a curt laugh through her tears.

"If it will make you feel better." He tilted her

face to his. "She's too valuable to kill. Kasdeya will want something in trade."

"I hope you're right." She pulled back and took a deep breath. "Let's keep looking until Linette calls us back." Which would come much too soon. Shayna glanced at the darkening sky, so dark she couldn't tell if it were afternoon or evening. The light extinguished more with each day. The end was coming.

Kasdeya

"Get your hands off me." The girl yanked free of Kasdeya's grasp and plastered her back against the opposite wall of the abandoned apartment.

"Hush." Kasdeya sneered and stood in front of the boarded-up window. Through a hole in one of the boards she watched as the faeries and humans searched for the girl. Kasdeya couldn't stay there. She had to find a way to Abaddon. He would be pleased with her gift.

Using the girl to trade for Radella and the captured demon would show Kasdeya's loyalty. She'd risked a lot coming into the open after the child.

Alvar's creatures couldn't regain their tolerance to heat, not with their increased size. She laughed.

The traitorous faerie had failed, leaving Kasdeya to be the victor. The faeries had an antidote to the poison coating the beast's claws. The vampire, Dan, was undisciplined, killing more humans than he turned. No one other than Radella could control him.

"What do you want with me?" the child's voice shook. "Let me go or I'll scream."

"Scream and I'll kill you and throw your broken body to the sidewalk below along with your precious bow." Kasdeya glanced at the bow and quiver in the corner.

"You aren't as bad as you think you are." She sniffed.

"Why do you say that?"

"I heard Detective Marshal talking to Deema. He thinks you can be saved." Her chin rose in defiance. "I don't."

"Really?" Interesting. Why would the man care? She turned back to the window. Handsome and strong-willed, he was her favorite if she had to choose one. If she could find a way of getting him to let go of his humanity, she'd do so without a second thought. Life was too lonely with no one to trust.

"I need to use the bathroom."

"I don't care." Kasdeya folded her hands behind her back and remembered the time before she'd chosen the dark. A time when the man she'd loved most in the world had failed her. The time he'd tied her to a sacrificial altar as a gift to his god.

Abaddon had come to her and offered her eternity in exchange for total obedience. Until recently, she'd thought she'd made the right choice. But power could still be hers if she made the right choices.

She turned to the child and gripped her by the arm before pulling a knife from her belt. "Not a sound, my child." She dragged her out the door and down a set of concrete and steel steps to the alley behind the building.

"My mother is going to put a spell on you and kill you." The child spit in her face.

"Insolent brat. I cannot be killed." Not easily, anyway, and not by a witch's spell.

Deema

"Stop." Deema held up a closed fist. "Kasdeya is close. My skin crawls with the evil emanating from her."

"Does she have Hanna?" Clark asked.

"I believe so." Deema raced for the alley, catching a glimpse of red as Kasdeya pulled the girl around a corner. "Cut them off. They are headed north." Without seeing whether the others obeyed, she continued the chase down the alley.

A clattering overhead drew her attention in time to see Kasdeya shove Hanna through an open window, then follow. She snarled before slamming a window shut.

Deema teleported to the top of the fire escape and shattered the window with the hilt of her sword. "You can't escape. Give yourself up."

"Not a chance." Kasdeya darted through an open door, her footsteps thundering as she sprinted away.

Deema climbed through the window, careful of the glass, and continued the chase. She stopped in the hallway and looked both ways. Which direction? She listened, then turned to her left, following Hanna's screams. Rounding a corner, she came face-to-face with the rest of her group.

"Where?" Shayna turned, glancing up and down the hall.

"I thought they would have passed you." Deema groaned.

A scream from behind another door. "You men, go through there. Shayna and I will teleport to the alley and street." With a shower of sparks, Deema arrived in front of the building to view a vacant street. A telepathic message to Shayna revealed the demon and child were not in the alley. They'd escaped, and dawn broke over the horizon.

Shayna approached from the opposite direction, shoulders squared, head up. "We have to go, as much as it pains us. The good news is that Hanna is alive. We will get her back."

"We will." Clark took Deema's hand. "Go to your queen. We'll do what we can here and join you later." He gave her a quick, hard kiss. "I love you, Deema. Take care of yourself."

She nodded and teleported to the Portal. Before

stepping through, she turned to Shayna. "I'm not staying. I will show myself to Linette, then sneak away. I'm tired of rules when action is better served."

"I'll come with you."

"No. The queen will be suspicious if we are both gone. You devise a plan to rid the world of Kasdeya so we can act once I find her." She stepped through the portal and into The Glen.

The decision she'd made would affect her future in the city of faeries. Still, she knew what had to be done and intended to do it, regardless. Not only would she find the child, but she would make sure she had a future with Clark. She cut a quick glance over her shoulder at Shayna. The serious expression on the other faerie's face said more than words. Shayna wouldn't stay behind when Deema left. Which meant Deema would truly have to sneak away.

Deema shoved open the doors to the throne room and entered. Shayna stepped to her side. Together, they approached the two sitting on their thrones.

Bowing her head, Deema said, "We found them, but were unable to rescue the girl. Kasdeya has escaped with her." She longed to ask for permission to keep seeking but wanted to avoid disobeying a direct order even more.

"We will send scouts," Linette said. "The child will not be left to the whim of Abaddon. The two of you are needed in the witch's tower."

Curses. Deema couldn't leave when she was expected elsewhere.

"Do not fear, my friend." Shayna clapped her on the shoulder. "We will go to the tower, then leave at the first opportunity."

"Just I."

"No, I read your face clearly and I won't let you go alone."

Deema faced her. "The risk to your reputation is great. I cannot allow it."

"It is not your place to allow or deny me anything." Shayna led the way up the tower steps. "I care deeply for Hanna and will not stay behind." She put a hand on the door and paused. "We must instill hope in Rachel."

"Hanna is alive, so there is hope." Deema reached for the doorknob. "She doesn't need to know the queen doesn't want us to keep looking."

Shayna sighed and opened the door.

Rachel rushed toward them. "My daughter?"

"Is alive." Deema forced a smile. "Kasdeya captured Hanna but hasn't harmed her. We will continue the search."

Rachel searched their faces, then nodded. "My girl is smart. She'll escape." She turned back to the table. "Then, she will face my wrath at her foolishness."

"She only wishes to help," Deema said. "Hanna is young, but not a small child. She has a warrior's heart."

Rachel spun, anger and fear etched on her face. "And I possess a mother's heart. She has no right to worry me. Bring my child home."

Deema met Shayna's gaze and shrugged. "I will not return until she is freed."

22
Shayna

"You cannot promise that." Shayna hurried to follow Deema down the stairs. "We can search, but we can't stay away until she is brought home. There's a battle fast approaching."

Deema whirled, her face inches from Shayna's. "Do you think I don't know that?" She slapped her chest. "I. Am. A. Warrior. Same as you. I know what's coming, and what we'll be risking."

"Then don't make promises you might not be able to keep." Shayna stormed down the stairs.

Deema grabbed her arm. "I intend to do a lot more than make promises I can't keep."

"You mustn't." Shayna followed her friend down the stairs. "There is no turning back from binding."

"I know."

"Stop. Please." Shayna shoved the other woman

against the side of a building. "Listen to me." She stared into the angry eyes of her friend. "I feel the same, but now is not the time. Do you want it to be a hurried, forbidden act or one of love?" Tears burned her throat. "Don't you know I feel the same for Pierce? I want our union to be a tender one."

"I just want the union." Deema pushed her back. "You do what you must, and I'll do what I must." She stormed away.

"I hope Clark Payson has more sense than you!" Shayna glared after Deema, then sprinted to follow her through the portal. Right or wrong, she couldn't let Deema go alone to rescue Hanna. She sent a message to Earin, letting him know where they'd gone and to fetch her if the city came under attack.

He roared back that she was an idiot and the queen would have her flogged. It didn't matter. Maybe Linette would change her mind about who she wanted her successor to be. Either way, irritated or not, Earin would come if asked.

"Leave me be." Deema shot a glare over her shoulder. "You don't need to be in trouble over my actions."

"I'm boss of my own mind." Shayna dogged her friend's steps. "Where are we headed?"

"Underground. If I were a demon, that's where I'd go. They have a fondness for the bowels of hell." Deema stopped at the entrance to the subway. "You really don't have to do this. The Glen needs you."

"They need both of us. The sooner we finish this, the better." Shayna switched to her armor. "Lead the way."

She spotted the first arrow at the bottom of the steps, the second in the center of the train tracks. Good girl. Hanna left them breadcrumbs of a sort. Without speaking, Shayna pointed at the arrow.

Deema grinned and set off at a run, collecting the arrows as she went deeper into the tunnels.

The subway tunnel was eerily quiet. No trains, no crowds, only a deep darkness that left a foul stench in the air. Could Abaddon have been this close all along?

Shayna stayed close to her friend's side, her gaze searching the shadows. Something didn't feel right. Dropped arrows, no guards…where were the vampires and other followers of the undead? A chill that had nothing to do with the temperature trickled down her spine. They shouldn't be searching alone. The two of them would be no match for an attack. Still, despite the cloud of dread hanging over her head, they moved further and further down the tracks, leaving any who could assist them behind.

How many arrows had Hanna kept in her quiver, she wondered as she watched Deema retrieve the tenth one. Twenty? Thirty? Where would they look when no more arrows littered the track?

"I can feel your questions," Deema whispered. "They're distracting." She stopped and stared at a partially opened door in the wall.

Shayna held her palm flat against the metal. "They came this way." She glanced at the iron track. "Already I feel the weakness seeping into my bones. We should have waited for Agatha and the others to complete the protection we needed."

"Hanna might not have that long." Deema pushed open the door.

Taking a deep breath, Shayna continued after her. The chase was folly. If they were attacked among the iron tracks, they'd perish, and Hanna's life would be forfeited.

As if he were summoned, arriving right when they needed him as he so often did, Earin teleported next to them. "Don't question, just drink. A gift from Agatha. It won't make you immune to iron, but will help give you some resistance. Agatha said not to be in such a hurry to leave next time." He handed Shayna a crystal bottle of light pink liquid. "I cannot stay. Someone must be available to lead our troops when you perish on this fool's errand." He glared his displeasure and left.

"Bless that witch." Shayna drank half the potion and handed the rest to Deema.

Strengthened, they continued their search, reaching a tunnel not built by human hands. Shayna took a deep breath and squared her shoulders. This was it. It had to be. Abaddon's dwelling under the human world. She grasped Deema's hand. "We live or die together."

"Agreed." Deema withdrew her sword. "But, I sure hope we take some demons and undead with us."

Deema

Deeper and deeper they went until the air turned cold as ice, then as hot as a furnace. They were close. She eyed the silver chain around Shayna's waist. Not nearly thick enough to bind the leader of the undead. They'd have to rescue Hanna and escape before they themselves were captured or killed.

A gate of iron bars stopped them a few yards further. While it didn't freeze their progression, it was enough to stop them. They could go no further, even with the potion they'd drunk. Defeat caused her to stumble. They'd come so far, only to fail.

"Can you hear anything?" She asked, straining her ears.

"Just a far-off mumbling." Shayna leaned against the dirt wall. "He is there. I can feel his evil."

"Hanna? Kasdeya?"

Shayna nodded. "I sense the girl's presence. I feel discord emanating from this tunnel. Abaddon is angry."

"Good. Maybe he'll kill his favorite demon." Deema backed away from the gate, studying the walls for another way in.

"No, that will leave Hanna at his mercy."

"Then what?" Must Shayna always be so serious?

"We enlist the men's help. They can go where we can't." Shayna headed back in the direction they'd come.

Almost a full day wasted. Another night fell, according to a nearby clock, and an innocent, willful child remained in the clutches of a demon. If they didn't find a way to save her, Linette wasn't the only one who would want payment for their leaving.

Once again, they came close to their goal only to turn back. Deema wished with everything in her that they could have ended the darkness at the last battle. The one looming in the future would be twice as deadly. Those who followed the Light had to win. There could be no other outcome. She mentally let Earin know where Abaddon abided. She didn't expect the undead leader to remain in that spot, but it might get the faeries a bit closer to capturing him.

At the precinct the men listened in stunned silence as she explained where they'd gone and what they'd discovered.

Pierce folded his hands on his desk. "You want us to go down there? I'm the only one who possesses any magic at all, and very little at that."

"We need someone not affected by iron to keep an eye out in case Abaddon leaves. Not for you to engage them." Deema crossed her arms.

"You want us to face the devil." Marshal paced the bull pen. "Yeah, that sounds like a real good time. What's to stop him from turning us into demons like Kasdeya?"

"Nothing. She isn't your typical demon,"

Deema said, smiling. "He only took away her humanity."

"Well, that's a relief."

"I thought you had a soft spot for her."

"It doesn't mean I want to be like her, only save her." He rolled his eyes. "What now, Chief?"

Pierce shrugged. "I guess we do surveillance." He glanced at Shayna. "You've been quiet, sweetheart. What's on your mind?"

"The more I think about it, the more I believe it might be a trap."

"How so?" Deema frowned.

"Kasdeya isn't stupid enough to let Hanna drop her arrows without knowing about it. She laid them there for us to find."

"To what end?" Clark raised his eyebrows. "She would know the iron would stop you."

Deema stiffened. Could Kasdeya be helping them? "It doesn't make sense. We stood near the gate for several minutes. No one attacked us. If it were a trap, we would have been swarmed with undead."

"I told you there was something about that woman in red that doesn't seem as bad as you say." Marshal plopped into his chair. "I do think she's helping us. The question is why?"

"Exactly. Why?" Deema emphasized the question. "She has no reason to help us. She hates those who follow the Light."

He grinned. "Maybe she hates Abaddon and Alvar more."

Deema jerked a glance at Shayna. "Could it be?"

"I don't know what to believe anymore," Shayna said. "At this point, anything seems possible. If Alvar truly is trying to take her place at Abaddon's side, she might want to sabotage him. But thinking she wants to join us is a long stretch indeed."

"But not impossible." Marshal's gaze hardened.

Deema didn't understand the man's fixation on Kasdeya. What had she ever done to lead him to believe she still had a heart that could be softened? She'd reigned for years with too much power to step down willingly. "You dream too much, Marshal. You're bound to be hurt in the end."

"My pain." He glanced around the room. "Are we heading to the tunnel or not?"

"We are." Pierce stood and grabbed his jacket and weapon. "Deema and Shayna will go with us as far as they can. After that, well, let's hope we live to see tomorrow as humans and not undead."

Kasdeya

Kasdeya knelt in front of Abaddon and stared at the hem of his black robe. The handsome man she'd vowed to serve stared down at her in scorn. When had things changed for her so horribly?

"What am I to do with a human child?" His

deep voice thundered over her.

"I thought you could trade her for the release of Radella and the other." She peered up from under lowered lashes. "Alvar's constant use of magic in order to strengthen his creatures is weakening him. He will fall long before the final battle."

"That is not your concern. At least he has the ability to do more than bark orders at vampires who don't obey."

"That's why I thought this girl useful. So you could get Radella back. They listen to her."

"Then what use are you to me?"

"My liege, I've been nothing but faithful." So, the feeling she had was true. Alvar had replaced her as Abaddon's favorite. She had no more worth in his eyes.

"I want you gone from my sight. I should never have taken a human and had her rule by my side." He got up from the iron throne and circled her. "Perhaps if you were to get Radella released, I could reconsider." He tilted her face to his.

She fought to keep her feelings from showing on her face. "That would be impossible. I cannot enter The Glen in this state."

"Alvar has found a way for his fantastic creatures to be in his land."

"But they cannot enter the lands possessed by Queen Linette."

He grinned without humor. "Then, I release you back to your human form. Be gone and take the brat with you." He planted his palm flat on her forehead and shoved her back hard enough to lift her feet from the floor and slam her into the wall next to where the girl huddled in fear. "You are now a human again." He laughed. "No power, no right to lead. Go and let the faeries send your soul to hell. Let the undead feast on the child. I care not. Alvar, even weak, has accomplished more for me than you ever did."

Kasdeya took the girl's hand. "Come," she whispered. "Don't say a word if you want to survive this day." As they moved slowly past Abaddon, every bone in Kasdeya's body ached, but she did her best to look subservient. "I will show you my worth again, my liege."

His laughter followed them into the tunnels.

Kasdeya tightened her grip. "Run, child. As fast and as far as you can. Find Shayna. Only she can protect you now." When the child hesitated, Kasdeya gave her a shove before crawling into the shadows to rest or die. She no longer cared which.

23
Shayna

Shayna led the others to the entrance of the tunnel where they last knew Abaddon to be. No foul stench floated in the air. No sense of overwhelming evil. "He is no longer here."

"No!" Deema darted down the tunnel.

Earin appeared next to them. Blood poured down his face from a gash in his head. "The palace has been attacked. The queens are missing. You must come."

Shayna's heart leaped into her throat. "Deema, we have to go." As soon as the other faerie returned, her dark eyes wide in her pale, tense face, they joined hands and teleported to madness and chaos. Bloodied warriors darted to and fro.

Smoke rose above the once-grand palace. Bodies of both light and dark-haired faeries littered the ground. The moans of the wounded filled the air.

"What happened?" Shayna blinked away the tears blurring her vision.

"Alvar. He came in disguise. No one realized it was him until a bolt from his fingers caused the palace roof to cave in." Earin bent over, clutching his side. "When that happened, the protective shield was destroyed, and his demons flooded the place."

"The queens?" She put a hand on his shoulder. "You said missing?"

"I don't know other than they're buried in the rubble." He swayed on his feet.

Pierce rushed forward and put a strong arm around the faerie, leading him to a nearby bench. "Sit, my friend. Just for a moment."

Deema spun him around. "Radella?"

Earin shrugged, his face paling. "We need to find the queens, not an undead who is most likely gone."

"We will find them. Deema, you run for the dungeon. See what we're dealing with. Pierce?" Shayna met his worried gaze.

"We'll help you dig." He motioned for the other two detectives to follow him.

Shayna located a few warriors still able to stand and ordered them to help the wounded to the infirmary. She shook her head when Earin wanted to stay. The dead would have to be left where they lay until the queens were found and those needing medical attention were in a place of safety.

She raised her hands and shot light from her palms, starting the slow, laborious task of moving huge chunks of marble from the palace floor and setting them in a vacant place near the training grounds. Sweat poured from her pores. She blinked the moisture away and fought through the weariness threatening to overtake her.

The queens were far more important than her fading strength. She couldn't stop, no matter how tired she grew. While she worked on the larger pieces, the men threw aside smaller chunks.

Deema hurried to her side and pressed Shayna's arms down. "Radella and the demon are gone, their chains broken. Since demons cannot be here unless brought by one of us, Alvar had to be the one who set them free. The circle of holy water had been swept clean."

"We can't search for them now. We must find the queens." Shayna's strength rose on the wings of anger. A muscle twitched near her right eye. She would be the one to kill Alvar as she stared into his traitorous face. There would be nowhere in either world where he could hide. "Help us dig or help the wounded."

Deema frowned. "I can search for him."

"Alvar is mine." An aggressive sweep of her hands sent a piece of marble crashing into another with a loud thunk.

"I'll help you dig." Deema raised her hands and started the same process of magically moving the larger pieces.

"Over here." Pierce pulled Brigette from the rubble. "She's still breathing."

From the look of her battled face, just barely. The queen's left arm hung at a strange angle, a bone protruding through the skin.

"I'll take her." Payson held out his arms. With a glance to where Shayna and Deema worked, he moved away as fast as he could while carrying the heavy weight of a faerie.

"Here's Linette." Marshal dragged the other queen from under a large beam.

Shayna rushed to the side of her queen. She lay her cheek against the ripped bodice of Linette's gown. A faint heartbeat sounded like music to her ears. "She lives but has lost a lot of blood." Her gaze traveled along the queen's body. "But I doubt she'll walk again." One leg crushed, the other missing below the knee. "Tie a tourniquet and get her to the infirmary. Tomorrow, we hunt for Alvar."

Once the injured were in the infirmary and the dead laid aside for burial, Shayna stepped under the waterfall near the mountain and let her soiled clothes fall to ground. She stared through the curtain of water as they were washed into the lake, then fell to her knees and let the pain and anger pour out of her in tears and screams hidden by the roaring of the water.

"Darling." Pierce stepped through the water and pulled her into his arms. "It will be okay. I'm here, your queen lives, the dark cannot win."

"They're cutting us apart with wounds that can never heal." She sobbed against his chest.

"You can't think that way." He tilted her face to his. "You are the light that leads us. Every one of us. You have taught us to fight, taught us where to lay our faith, and taught me how to love."

She ran her hands down his arms, plucking at the sodden fabric of his suit jacket. "Then bind with me. Here. Now. I will never want another. If you perish, I'll remain alone for the rest of my life. If I perish—"

He put a hand to her lips. "But the queen—"

"Cannot reign for a long while, which puts me in control, and the first law I said I would change was this one." She smiled and raised on the tips of her toes, wrapping her arms around his neck. "A queen no longer needs to remain single. A fae can choose for themselves who to bind with. I choose you. Please, so we may be together for as long as we may have left."

He scooped her into his arms and grinned. "Then I say we find a soft patch of moss, my love."

Deema

Deema sat beside Brigette's bed and wiped the queen's forehead with a cool cloth. "You're lucky, you and Linette."

"How is she?"

"Alive, same as you, although she's been put into a medical coma for her injuries. She won't walk again."

"My heart breaks at the news. We were stupid." Brigette pushed to a sitting position and grimaced. "Alvar entered through a side entrance, a cloak covering his features. The guards at the door had been killed. Before Linette and I knew who he was, the roof started to fall. By then it was too late." She gripped Deema's hand. "He said Kasdeya had been banished, and he was now Abaddon's right hand. He oozed evil. He must be stopped."

"The crystal ball?"

"He made no mention of it, but he had to have known Linette and I were alone in the throne room. I believe the ball is in his possession. The child?"

Deema shook her head. "We haven't seen her."

Brigette lay back and closed her eyes. "Don't despair. It will all come together. It is always darkest before the morning. You reign in my place until I can do so again."

Tears stung Deema's eyes. "I will not stop looking for Hanna."

Brigette smiled. "I know. Shayna has changed the law regarding binding. Go, my love and seek the man you love. One never knows what day will be their last. Go, love him, and pick up your sword again tomorrow."

Deema didn't have to be told twice. She found Clark washing the skinned knee of a child and watched from the sidelines as he then helped an elderly faerie to a cushion placed on the ground for her comfort.

Overhead, dragons circled, keeping their sharp eyes peeled for any sign of a new danger. With the collapse of the protective shield, their location was no longer secret. She put her gaze back on Clark.

He worked tirelessly along with Marshal, going from one mildly wounded or frightened person to the next. They offered comfort with a touch, a kind word, a clean rag. The three detectives were wonderful humans, and Deema would be forever grateful that Shayna had met Pierce in that alley. Good hearts, all three, and one of them held her heart in his calloused, gentle hands.

She couldn't pull him away from his ministrations for her own needs. They still had the night. For now, she'd hunt for Hanna.

She sprinted for the portal. Once through, she smiled, sensing the very one she sought. "Hanna?"

"Deema?" The child crawled from under a bush and launched into Deema's arms. "I couldn't get through. The portal was closed."

"Only for a while." It could no longer be left open on a permanent basis with Alvar knowing its location. This one would be closed like the last and another created. That one would be opened and closed as needed. Moving between the faerie world and the human one would no longer be as simple as stepping into the crevice of a large tree. "Let's take you home. Shayna will have many questions."

Once back through, Deema waved her hand and closed the portal. Then, taking the girl's hand in hers, she led Hanna to the tower to reunite with her mother.

"Mom." Hanna barged through the door and flung herself at her mother.

"Oh, my darling. How did you get away?" Rachel hugged her, then held her at arm's length.

"Kasdeya set me free. Abaddon hurt her. She's a human again and hiding somewhere under New York. She never harmed me."

Deema turned as Shayna rushed toward them. The other faerie emanated more light than before, still glowing from her binding time with Pierce. A flicker of envy rose in Deema's heart, only to be snuffed out. Smiling, she backed from the room and went again to find Clark.

This time, he sat on a chunk of marble, head bowed, hands hanging between his legs. Exhaustion bowed his shoulders. It wasn't until she took his hand that she realized he'd fallen asleep sitting up.

"Come." She cupped his face. "Let us bathe and love, for weariness coats your features. You've done well for today."

His eyes brightened. "That's the best thing I've heard in a long time." He glanced to where Pierce stood with Marshal. "We're all tired."

Deema laughed. "I think Pierce least of all." She pulled him to his feet. "A bath, food, and binding, sir, in that order."

He laughed. "Let's switch the order up. I'll bathe first, but food can wait." Lowering his head, he kissed her.

24
Deema

Deema stood to the right of Shayna at the dinner table and looked over the faces of those gathered there, Pierce, Clark, Marshal, Earin and the witches. Content to let Shayna take over as sole queen, she'd set herself up as leader of the fighters. With Linette's passing during the night, Shayna was no longer the stand-in for the queen, but queen herself.

"The darkness is coming to The Glen. Already it approaches on the wind. Our fight is no longer just in the human world." She clasped her hands in front of her. "You all are our core fighting group. On your shoulders weighs the outcome of this war. Yes, we are few, but we are strong and full of light. The leprechauns, sprites, gnomes, and a few giants have pledged to fight with us." She scanned each face at the table with fierce intent. "Some of us, along with our allies, will fall on the battlefield. Alvar may seem strong after yesterday's destruction, but he grows weaker. Our focus must be on Abaddon."

"What about Kasdeya?" Marshal asked.

Shayna stood. "According to Hanna, she is injured and in hiding. Her fate is not our concern."

His face darkened. "Isn't the life of every human important? You said something to that effect once. Capturing Kasdeya would give us inside information on Abaddon and Alvar. I think that would be of great importance."

Deema glanced from him to Shayna. "As surprised as I am to say so, I agree. Kasdeya could be a great asset."

"We can't trust her." Shayna shook her head. "What if she betrays us to Abaddon?"

"I say we try." Marshal tossed his napkin onto his half-empty plate.

Pierce nodded. "If we keep her under close watch, it might work to our advantage."

Deema put a hand on Shayna's arm to stop her protest. "Find her, Marshal. She will be your responsibility. If she tries to betray us, it will be your hand that holds the sword to end her life. Understand?"

"I do." He rushed from the room, shouting, "Close the portal in twenty minutes and open it every evening at dusk for fifteen."

Deema fell back into her chair. "He will not return without her."

"No." Shayna glanced at Agatha. "Can we track him?"

"Oh, honey, I put a tracker on everyone in this

group days ago." She grinned. "We'll know when he approaches the portal and needs entry. When will you stop doubting my ability to know what is needed?"

Shayna laughed. "It seems I need constant reminding." She resumed her seat. "Although I am reigning queen, each of us will be on that battlefield when the time comes. Everyone with the ability to lift a sword or cast a spell will be there. The warriors still healing will stay behind in the caves with the women and children. If we lose, our race will still go on until all are consumed by darkness. Any questions?"

"That means my son will fight?" Rachel's shoulders slumped.

"Only the oldest one. He is already in training." Deema put a hand on the woman's shoulder. "It must be this way."

"Can he not stay behind with his learned skills to protect the others?"

"No. He has requested to go. As a fifteen-year-old male, he will be a great fighter. Use your skill to protect him in every way you can."

"I'm working on something to make Alvar's magic useless against us," Agatha said, pushing to her feet. "Let the magic come only from our side. There is nothing fair in war."

"Our own training resumes at dawn." Deema gave a definitive nod. "I will personally see to your son's training."

"Then I will worry no more." Rachel stood and left, followed by the other witches.

Deema meant what she said. She wouldn't let

the boy fall while she drew a breath. She studied the faces of her friends. Not one of them would die before her. She gripped Shayna's hand and held it high. "Long live Queen Shayna."

"Hear! Hear!" Voices and glasses raised. "Long live Queen Shayna."

Shayna

This time there would be no returning of the staff she held in her hand. Shayna was queen. She stared through tears at the beloved faces across from her. She could only hope to do them justice as ruler and find someone to replace her should she and Deema perish.

With Pierce at her side, she left the dining hall and made the rounds of the wounded at the infirmary. Those who stood bowed, those who couldn't nodded. Those were what remained of her people. So many warriors dead.

Pierce took her hand, lending his support.

"You are bound to the queen," she said, smiling through her sadness. "That makes you the second most important person in The Glen. Help me choose my successor."

"Hopefully you'll soon carry one in your womb, but I grasp your meaning. I'll help you decide." He gave her hand a gentle squeeze.

"It puts a large target on your back." She cut him a sideways glance, her steps not faltering as she returned each nod from one of her subjects.

"I've a strong back."

So he did, her warrior chief of police. "Who is running the precinct?"

"Officer Charges. It's a lot of responsibility for one so young, but he's got good men fighting with him. He understands I'm needed at your side. I'll check in with him when I can."

After the infirmary, they strolled among the ruins of the palace. A queen without a throne. A queen with an army she could count on her fingers and toes. She squared her shoulders. As long as the light flickered inside of them, they were an army to be reckoned with. All hope was not lost.

The work of rebuilding had begun. What marble could be salvaged would be used to erect new walls, the shattered pieces became a path or part of a floor. A new shield of protection had been erected over the city. With the portals kept closed, the city was safe unless Alvar found a new way in. A new determination to lure Alvar to where the side of the Light wanted him rose in her heart. Never again would this city be attacked. Not while she lived.

She ducked into the tent she shared with Pierce to find Earin sitting on a stool. He leaped to his feet at the sight of her and bowed.

"At ease. Did you partake of refreshment? I didn't see you at dinner." Shayna poured three glasses of faerie wine, a delicacy set aside for the royals to enjoy. She smiled at the surprised look on

Pierce's face. She'd fallen into the pattern of less formal speech while in his world, but felt one in her place should speak as a queen would. Or perhaps not. It would grow very tiresome.

"I ate, my queen. Marshal had me close the portal. Has he deserted us?"

"No, he has gone to capture Kasdeya. She may have knowledge that will be of use to us." Shayna handed him and Pierce a goblet. "Please, sit."

She sat on a woven straw chair covered with a lush blue blanket. "Is that all?"

"My wounds are healing. I don't want to be left behind when we fight."

"You won't." She smiled. "How can I leave one of my best warriors behind? We need you fighting at our side." It had been a while coming, but Earin no longer held the prejudices he once had of fighting next to humans and leprechauns. "While Deema is now in charge of our fighters, you are sorely needed at her side."

"A pleasure, my queen." He sipped his wine, something clearly still on his mind.

"Speak."

He took a deep breath. "Permission to court Becky."

Shayna choked. "A witch?"

His cheeks reddened, and he cast a glance at Pierce. "I'm drawn to her."

Pierce laughed. "She is a pretty woman. Go in the Light, my friend. Shayna cannot deny you what she herself has chosen to do."

"Thank you." He set his goblet on a table and backed from the tent.

"People never cease to surprise, do they?" Shayna drank.

"When you fight next to someone, rely on them to keep you safe, it changes things." He leaned forward to kiss her. "Did I step over any boundaries by granting him permission?"

"No, I asked you to rule at my side." She smiled into his eyes. "A team, you and I, to rule this world until we close our eyes for the last time."

"The coming days will be tough."

She nodded. "I can handle them with you."

"You're right about losing people."

Pain stabbed her heart. "We've already lost Linette, and almost Brigette who has stepped down from the throne saying she wishes to spend the rest of her life doing whatever she wants when she wants to."

"There is a lot of restriction put on a person of power."

She sighed. "I know better than most."

Kasdeya

Kasdeya crawled from the hole she'd lain in for two days and tested her bruised ribs. A gasp escaped her at a sharp pain in her side. Her stomach rumbled with hunger, a feeling she hadn't felt in a long time. Cotton filled her mouth from lack of water. She shuffled down the tunnel, emerging onto the subway tracks. Not seeing anyone, she headed down the way she had yet to explore.

Eventually, she'd come across a person or a place where she could receive aid. Until then, one foot in front of the other would be the chant she repeated past every painful breath. She cursed Abaddon, Alvar, and the rest. Kasdeya had sacrificed everything for them, only to be thrown aside like a crumpled newspaper already read.

No matter what, she'd make sure they all paid. She leaned against the subway wall to catch her breath. Had the child had made it to safety? Hopefully, if the girl told Shayna how Kasdeya had helped her escape, the faerie would have mercy if the two of them came face-to-face. She doubted the faerie would allow her to live, so all she could hope for was a merciful and swift death. Hope. Ha. As if she'd had any to begin with.

"Kasdeya!"

She whirled to see Marshal standing on the platform. "Go away. I'm no longer a threat to you." She stumbled away from the wall.

"Let me help you."

She broke into a limping run, then clamored up a ladder to the surface as his footsteps pounded behind her. Why would he want to help her? She'd done despicable things to his people.

Outside, she glanced at a sky swirling with dark clouds. The few people who were out scurried, heads down, intent on reaching their destination before harm fell upon them. She wanted to yell to them all to stay inside with their doors locked. To paint their doors and windows with silver, but she had to keep going. Marshal was gaining on her.

The End

Stay tuned for book three, **Kasdeya**. The war is coming.

Kasdeya

Kasdeya scrambled up a ladder in the subway to the street above and merged with the crowd. She couldn't be captured. Not yet. She had to live long enough to get revenge on Abaddon. A quick glance behind her showed Marshal quickly gaining. Before she'd been reverted to human form, before her injuries, she could have left the man far behind her. No longer. Now she was nothing more than a mere mortal, with all the setbacks that came with it.

"Just listen to me." Marshal raced after her.

"Help me." Kasdeya gripped the arm of a large man next to her. "Stop him. He'll hurt me."

While the stranger blocked Marshal's path, Kasdeya ducked into a corner café and out the back door. With a quick glance both ways, she chose right and sprinted down the alley, one arm pressed to her battered ribcage.

Coming back onto the busy New York street, she continued her flight. With no money and no food, her only option was a women's shelter a few blocks over. That or a church. She was pretty sure God wouldn't let her step one toe inside His house. Women's shelter it was.

She barged through the double doors and leaned against the wall, struggling to catch her breath against the pain in her side. A middle-aged woman rushed to help Kasdeya into a chair.

"Oh, dear." She snapped her fingers at a

younger woman. "Get the doctor." She turned back to Kasdeya. "Who hurt you, honey? Do you want me to call the police? What's your name?"

Too many questions. "No police, thank you. The man who…mugged me is long gone. My name is Kassy."

"Come on, let's get you taken care of, fed, and cleaned up." She helped Kasdeya to a back room and handed her a towel. "Shower is right through there. Just wrap the towel around you so the doctor can get a good look at your injuries. I'll be right here if you need me. Are you hungry?"

Kasdeya nodded on her way to the shower. She stripped down and laid her red leather jacket and pants on a nearby stool. They'd need cleaning but would have to go to a dry cleaner. She could change into something else, but the leather made her feel fierce, and she'd worn it for a very long time. So long it had become like a second skin to her.

Closing her eyes, she stepped under the hot spray of the shower and let the water wash away the grime from the tunnels and ease some of the aching from her shoulders. Tears rolled down her cheeks, disappearing down the drain with the water. If only she'd killed the child. Then, she'd still be Abaddon's right hand and powerful. Her heart wasn't as dark as people believed after all.

After her shower, a strange woman waited in the next room. "I'm Doctor Clark. Sit on this cot and let me take a look at you. Doris brought you a dress."

"I'd like to wear the red." Kasdeya sat, turning a suspicious gaze on the doctor. Learning to trust humans again would take some time.

"Let's at least get it cleaned, shall we?" The doctor listened to her heart, her lungs, then had her lie back so she could gently press her ribcage. "I suspect you have some fractures but no hard breaks. That is good. I'll wrap you up and tend to your scrapes. Would you like to tell me what happened?"

"I betrayed a powerful man."

The doctor made a disgusted sound in her throat. "That will get you beat up every time. My advice to you is to stay away from him."

Kasdeya nodded, intending anything but staying away. Once she found a way to destroy the leader of the dead, she'd make sure he joined those who blindly followed him into hell. When the doctor left, giving her something for the pain, Kasdeya donned the simple red and yellow sundress, then lay back and fell asleep.

Marshal

Where could she have gone? Marshal stood on the street corner, hands on his hips, and glared at the big brute who'd stopped him. "I ought to arrest you for obstruction of justice."

The man held up his hands. "I had no idea you were a cop." The grin on his face and the tone of his voice sounded as if it wouldn't have mattered. His actions would have been the same if he'd known Marshal was law enforcement.

Marshal groaned. In a city the size of New

York, a city where the sky darkened with each day and undead roamed the streets, Kasdeya could be anywhere. "Get inside, dude. Haven't you heard? It's not safe on the streets anymore."

"Yeah, I heard about the vampires. Crazy stuff, but my kids got to eat." He shook his head and strolled away, slapping a hard hat on.

The man worked outside? He'd be joining the undead before the week was out if he didn't stay extra-vigilant. Marshal shoved his hands in his pockets and hurried to the portal.

Reconstruction from the traitor Alvar's attack was in full force on rebuilding the palace despite Queen Shayna's insistence that she'd rather rule her people under the sky and trees than in a marble palace, no matter how grand the building.

He located her on a makeshift throne placed under the drooping branches of a willow tree. At her side sat Pierce. The clang of swords proved Deema and Payson were hard at work on the training field. After the death of many warriors, new ones needed to be brought up for the approaching battle.

"No Kasdeya?" Shayna frowned.

"She convinced some brute of a man to step in front of me. By the time I got around him, she had disappeared. I'll head out again at dark." Not that the day wasn't already as dark as dusk.

He accepted a crystal goblet of water from a passing steward. "Before you say no, I understand the danger, but if she comes out of hiding, it will be under the cover of darkness. I've got my necklace." He pulled the cross from under his shirt. "My bottle of holy water and my sword. I'll be fine. I have a better chance of getting her to listen if I'm alone. If we approach her as a group, she'll see it as a sign of force and keep running."

"I still think she can't be trusted." Deema stopped next to them.

"I believe everyone should get a second chance." Shayna leaned forward. "Once she's caught, she is your responsibility, Marshal. You cannot let her betray us. Once she crosses the portal, she must be kept on a tight rein until her faithfulness is proven. The fact that she didn't kill Hanna is not enough proof for me that she is willing to change."

"I understand." His heart told him the former demon follower was no longer the same person, but his head agreed with Deema. He'd have to be careful. "How is Rachel's boy coming along in his training?"

Deema grinned. "With the same potion Agatha gave you three detectives, he's coming along surprisingly well. The young man is like a dancer on the battlefield. Yes, Logan will be an asset in a fight, even at the young age of fifteen." Her smile faded. "I'd like to say Kasdeya can't be changed, but I came back to the Light. If she proves her loyalty, I'll fight by her side." With those words, the faerie marched away.

He turned back to Shayna. "I just want her to have a chance."

"She will have one, but only one chance." Shayna smiled. "Go get some rest and eat. Go in the Light, Marshal. You've a good heart."

Maybe, but it hadn't always been that way.

When he'd first found out that faeries, demons, and the like existed outside the pages of a fairy tale, he'd been more than skeptical. He'd been angry and disillusioned at the rising crime and death rate in a world he loved. Now, having encountered demons and vampires face-to-face, gratitude to fight on the side of the Light filled him. At least the side he fought for had hope.

He sat at the end of a long table next to the training grounds and ate with the warriors. No matter how much Shayna called him one, he could never see himself as one of them. The faeries were ferocious in battle and fought without fear. Every time he lifted his sword, his knees almost buckled under the weight of his own fear. Still, they accepted him now as one of their own and welcomed him as he took his seat.

"I can send a fighter or two to help you in your search," Earin said, passing a plate of something blue.

Marshal had never tasted anything as good as what was served in The Glen, nor any food as brightly colored. "No, I'd best do this alone, but thanks." He finished eating, showered under the waterfall, and ducked back through the portal.

If he were a wounded, frightened woman who felt she had no one to trust, where would he go? He scoured the churches around the area he'd last seen Kasdeya, but no one had seen her. He hit pay dirt on the second women's shelter he located because the gray-haired general at the door would not allow him in.

"I'm a detective. I need to locate this woman for

her own protection." He showed his badge.

"Unless she's broken the law and you intend to arrest her, she is safer here." The woman crossed her arms.

They entered into a stare down. "I'll be back tomorrow with a warrant."

Alvar

Alvar rubbed his hands together. Getting rid of Kasdeya by convincing Abaddon she'd betray him over time was the best, most diabolical thing he'd ever done. Now he was the demon leader's right hand, not some human given immortality. A magical fae could do so much more in ridding the world of light.

He glanced to where Linc, the panther shapeshifter, lounged in front of a fire. The dark-skinned man, even in human form, seemed more like a cat than a man. "I need you to sniff her out," Alvar said. "Kasdeya must be destroyed. She knows too much." He ran his hand over the crystal ball he'd found near the old portal to The Glen. Little information came through, but he knew The Glen's occupants were rebuilding and training. If they recruited Kasdeya, things would veer in their favor.

"I'll go later," Linc said. "It's cold outside."

"Put on a jacket. Where's Radella?"

"I'm not her keeper." The man even had the temperament of a cat. If not for the luxury Alvar provided, the shifter would have no loyalty at all.

"I'm here." The beautiful vampire sashayed toward him and perched on the arm of the chair, handing him a whiskey and running her fingers through his hair. "What does my lord command?"

"My whiskey, then you in the bedroom, in that order." He smiled up at her. Since he'd freed her from the chains of The Glen's dungeon, she'd vowed undying loyalty and promised herself in return. Still, in bed, Alvar ordered her to wear a mouthpiece over her fangs. He might enjoy the vampire, but he didn't trust her not to bite during the throes of passion. She'd mentioned more than once she'd like to turn him.

He laughed. Power! The grandness of it. He had a powerful cat at his feet and a beautiful immortal woman on his arm. What more could a faerie ask for?

Dear Reader,

Are you enjoying these characters as much as I am? The world is always at battle between good and evil. All you have to do is watch the news to know this is true.

What if faeries really did fight forces for us that we could not fight ourselves? Oh, the scope of possibilities if such magical creatures existed. I hope this series transports you to a place where goodness runs rampant in the hearts of warriors, both fae and human.

If you enjoyed Deema, I would love for you to leave a review. Reviews are priceless to authors.

Go in the Light,

Cynthia Hickey

Connect with me on FaceBook
Twitter
Bookbub
Sign up for my newsletter and receive a free short story
www.cynthiahickey.com

Follow me on Amazon

Enjoy other books by Cynthia Hickey

Fantasy (written as Cynthia Melton)
Fate of the Faes
Shayna

Time Travel
The Portal

A Hollywood Murder
Killer Pose, book 1
Killer Snapshot, book 2
Shoot to Kill, book 3

Shady Acres Mysteries
Beware the Orchids, book 1
Path to Nowhere
Poison Foliage
Poinsettia Madness
Deadly Greenhouse Gases
Vine Entrapment

CLEAN BUT GRITTY

Highland Springs

Murder Live
Say Bye to Mommy
To Breathe Again

Colors of Evil Series

Shades of Crimson
Coral Shadows

The Pretty Must Die Series

Ripped in Red, book 1
Pierced in Pink, book 2
Wounded in White, book 3
Worthy, The Complete Story

Lisa Paxton Mystery Series

Eenie Meenie Miny Mo
Jack Be Nimble
Hickory Dickory Dock

One Hour (A short story thriller)

INSPIRATIONAL
(scroll down to see clean books without inspirational message)

Whisper Sweet Nothings (a short romance)

Nosy Neighbor Series

Anything For A Mystery, Book 1
A Killer Plot, Book 2
Skin Care Can Be Murder, Book 3
Death By Baking, Book 4
Jogging Is Bad For Your Health, Book 5
Poison Bubbles, Book 6
A Good Party Can Kill You, Book 7 (Final)
Nosy Neighbor collection

Christmas with Stormi Nelson

The Summer Meadows Series
Fudge-Laced Felonies, Book 1
Candy-Coated Secrets, Book 2
Chocolate-Covered Crime, Book 3
Maui Macadamia Madness, Book 4
All four novels in one collection

The River Valley Mystery Series
Deadly Neighbors, Book 1
Advance Notice, Book 2
The Librarian's Last Chapter, Book 3
All three novels in one collection

Historical cozy
Hazel's Quest

Historical Romances
Runaway Sue
Taming the Sheriff
Sweet Apple Blossom

Finding Love the Harvey Girl Way
Cooking With Love
Guiding With Love
Serving With Love
Warring With Love
All 4 in 1

A Wild Horse Pass Novel
They Call Her Mrs. Sheriff, book 1 (A Western Romance)

Finding Love in Disaster
The Rancher's Dilemma
The Teacher's Rescue
The Soldier's Redemption

Woman of courage Series

A Love For Delicious
Ruth's Redemption
Charity's Gold Rush
Mountain Redemption
Woman of Courage series (all four books)

Short Story Westerns
Desert Rose
Desert Lilly
Desert Belle
Desert Daisy
Flowers of the Desert 4 in 1

Romantic Suspense

Overcoming Evil series
Mistaken Assassin

DEEMA

Captured Innocence
Mountain of Fear
Exposure at Sea
A Secret to Die for
Collision Course
Romantic Suspense of 5 books in 1

The Game
Suspicious Minds

Contemporary

Romance in Paradise
Maui Magic
Sunset Kisses
Deep Sea Love
3 in 1

Finding a Way Home

Service of Love

Christmas

Handcarved Christmas
The Payback Bride
Curtain Calls and Christmas Wishes
Christmas Gold
A Christmas Stamp
Snowflake Kisses

The Red Hat's Club (Contemporary novellas)

Finally

CYNTHIA MELTON

Suddenly
Surprisingly
The Red Hat's Club 3 – in 1

Short Story

One Hour (A short story thriller)
Whisper Sweet Nothings (a Valentine short romance)

www.ingramcontent.com/pod-product-compliance
Lightning Source LLC
LaVergne TN
LVHW011812060526
838200LV00053B/3749